Wh
The Uni\

Anthony Grey
ANTHONY GREY

To James

with love and warmest good wishes — these are the very first pieces of fiction which led to SAIGON....

Tony
5 August 2003

TAGMAN
Worldwide

www.tagman-press.com

What is the Universe In ?

First published in Great Britain simultaneously in hardcover and paperback in the year 2003 by Tagman Worldwide (Ltd) in The Tagman Press imprint. An earlier hardback version of the stories in this volume A Man Alone, was first published by Michael Joseph Ltd, 32 Bedford Square, London WC1 in l971
The first paperback edition was published in l990 by Pan Books Ltd, Cavaye Place, London SW10 9PG

Tagman Worldwide (Ltd)
Lovemore House, 5 Caley Close,
Sweet Briar Estate,
Norwich NR3 2BU England UK
and 1888 Century Park East, Suite 1900
Los Angeles, CA 90067-1702 USA

Internet : www.tagman-press.com
e-mail : editorial@tagman-press.com

© Copyright 2003 by Anthony Grey

The right of Anthony Grey to be identified as the author of this work has been asserted by him in accordance with the Copyright, Designs and Patents Act 1988

All rights reserved. No part of this publication may be reproduced, stored in a retrieval system or transmitted in any form or by any means, electronic, mechanical, recording or otherwise, without the prior written permission of the author and copyright holder

ISBN   0-9530921-8-6 (hardback)
ISBN   1-903571-12-X (paperback)

A CIP catalogue record for this book is available from The British Library

The Tagman Press and the author are grateful for permission to quote passages from *The Trial* by Franz Kafka copyright 1937, 1956 and 1964, published by Alfred A Knopf Inc., reprinted by permission of Schocken Books Inc. who hold the copyright in Canada and Martin Secker & Warburg Ltd, who hold the copyright in the British Commonwealth

Edited and designed by Bill Wedge
Author's photograph: Paul Dickson, Isis Communications
Cover design: Kevin Jones, Hotbrand (www.hot-brand.com)

Printed by CLE Print Ltd, Media House, Burrel Road, St Ives, Huntingdon, Cambridgeshire PE27 3LE

TAGMAN
Worldwide

This republished volume is dedicated
with great love
and affection in the year 2003 to the memory of
my mother and father,
Agnes and Alfred Grey

Anthony Grey's novels, short stories and non-fiction books have been translated into some 16 languages worldwide. He is best known internationally for his enduring historical epics Saigon, Peking and Tokyo Bay which are critically acclaimed bestsellers in Britain, Europe, the Far East, South Africa, Australia, New Zealand and North and South America.

He became a foreign correspondent with Reuters after beginning a career in journalism with the Eastern Daily Press in Norwich where he was born and educated. He covered the Cold War from East Berlin and other East European capitals before being assigned to China. He was the sole Reuter correspondent based in Peking in 1967 and the only British journalist resident in the Chinese capital. He first came to world attention when he was taken hostage by Mao Tse-tung's Red Guards at the height of the Cultural Revolution. Held in solitary confinement for over two years, he was the first and most widely publicised political hostage of the Cold War era. After his release, his first book Hostage in Peking became a bestseller in seven countries. To date he has written eight novels.

During a broadcasting career he has written and presented television documentary films for BBC, ITV and Channel Four and presented daily current affairs programmes on BBC World Service Radio from Bush House in London. In 1998 he moved from London to Norfolk where he now lives and set up Tagman Worldwide (Ltd) in Norwich to publish books and multimedia audio-visual products which challenge conventional concepts in science, health and personal development. The Tagman Press imprint also publishes books on journalism.

Critical acclaim for the stories of What is the Universe In? when first published in 1971 as A Man Alone

'Without exception polished pieces of writing which make excellent reading'
Christchurch Press, New Zealand

'Thoroughly readable, sometimes moving, sometimes amusing and usually concerned with elemental themes: the brevity of human life or the strange tricks played by destiny ... Powerfully conceived.'
British Book News

'This book reveals a man, who, incredibly retains his sense of humour and remembers his home city with sensitivity and longing ... It gives a startling insight into his character and personality.'
Sunday Times, Wellington, New Zealand

'As the expression of a man in solitary confinement under the pressure of uncertainty and fear, these compositions possess a remarkable buoyancy.'
The Scotsman

'Since there is an obvious basic talent, the stories have a good deal of technical as well as personal interest'
The Guardian

'His stories are macabre fantasies, nightmares of reality, that are both extremely funny – and extremely frightening.'
The Birmingham Post

Reviews of Hostage in Peking

How a man can survive in a state of stunning emptiness and isolation, how stay alive in spirit as well as physically, is the essence of this exceptionally fine and memorable book...What Grey had to face was psychological pressure of a most insidious kind, and previous newspaper accounts have barely indicated a fraction of it... It is a book, in short, about a singular triumph of mind, one not to be missed.
The Observer (Roy Perrott)

His dispassionate report of his ordeal during two years of solitary confinement and his rueful record of an intelligent reporter's human reflexes and contrived responses to boredom and 'dripping water' torment make his work a fascinating modern addition to the world library of historic prison stories.
The Sunday Times (Richard Hughes)

Those who have read in the press of Anthony Grey's long and terrible ordeal must have wondered how a man could possibly survive it with his sanity intact. After reading this well-balanced and moving book they will wonder even more. It is written modestly, thoughtfully, and in an unassuming style, and leaves us with a better idea of what Grey endured than might have emerged from a more pretentious history. It is important that his book should be read in full to understand the nature of the regime in power in China today... One leaves his book remembering the sublime courage of a man, and the shame of a nation.
Daily Telegraph (The Earl of Birkenhead)

Perhaps people, who don't come close to losing it, don't appreciate the goodness of life. They should do after reading his book. Anthony Grey's story makes the grass grow greener...vivid and moving.
Sunday Express (Graham Lord)

A detailed, pungent and never wearisome description of his captivity in Peking... In many ways it is a vignette of a very remarkable and turbulent passage of Chinese history, repeated in a thousand ways albeit with different facts –and much more than a simple story of a journalist in solitary confinement... The book provides much insight into the events of the Cultural Revolution... It is likely to be a popular volume in the libraries of western countries for a very long time to come.
South China Morning Post, Hong Kong (W.V. Pennell)

Contents

		Page
AUTHOR'S PREFACE 2003		9
PROLOGUE		11
	Man Alone	13
1	HIMSELF	15
	What is the Universe In?	35
2	THE OLD MAN AND THE LEAVES	37
	Prayers Whispered into a Bath	47
3	TO CUT A LONG STORY SHORT	51
	The Play	60
4	GOLLYWHITE FOR SIGMUND	64
	The Moon and Storms	78
5	CRIME AND CALCULUS	80
	The Trial	96
6	NEWTON'S LORE OF GRAFFITI	99
	No Story	108
7	A MAN WAS LATER DETAINED	110
EPILOGUE		122
AUTHOR'S POSTSCRIPT 2003		133

Publisher's Introduction
to the 1971 edition of *A Man Alone*

This collection of short stories came out of Anthony Grey's experience while detained as a hostage in Peking. Isolated, imprisoned in a tiny room, he was indeed a man alone for two long years, two years in which he had nothing to do, nowhere to go, no one to talk to.

He has described that condition as a mental siege. All the resources of his mind had to rally to its defence. This they did and *A Man Alone* is one of the results.

The stories are waking dreams, imaginative excursions beyond the soul-destroying tedium of each day. But they are not sheer escapism. Anthony Grey was well aware of the dangers of daydreams, which destroy reality, leading possibly to insanity. His dreams were objective, a deliberate evocation of faraway places in England, but concerned with other people, with impersonal themes such as the renewal of life and strange quirks of fate. Above all they have an almost tangible feeling of place.

But although his position made him consider universal questions with an immediacy and awareness not felt by the busy and the preoccupied, his thoughts were by no means sombre. Humour as well as imagination aided him. Sometimes this bursts out in the downright ludicrous or the direct lampoon and Anthony Grey shows a pleasing touch of originality, particularly when he is taking us sailing down his own arteries and veins past both irreverent and responsible cells busily keeping 'Himself' alive.

A Man Alone is the companion to *Hostage in Peking*, the step-by-step account of Anthony Grey's imprisonment, which has been published in seven countries. *A Man Alone* deepens the picture already given of how a remarkable man survived.

Author's Preface
2003

Writing a new introduction for this re-titled collection of short stories and philosophical reflections some 35 years after they were first penned in China is a particular pleasure for me. There are several different reasons for this.

First, apart from anything else, they were my first published fictional stories. They proved to be the forerunners of the eight novels I have written to date in the succeeding three decades, the bridge, which I crossed, in expanding my horizons from international journalism to historical fiction and then much more recently to publishing.

Second and more importantly, though, the republication of these stories in this modern twenty-first century edition allows me to set them in a new historical context. This shows how they form an important and direct link between that strange experience of total isolation as a hostage in China in the late 1960s with my current view of the nature of the reality in which we live.

Re-birthing them now in this new edition gives me the opportunity to clarify the initially puzzling insights I gained in China without fully understanding them. They concern the place of our planet in relation to the rest of our known universe and beyond, the true nature of our inner selves and ultimately our vital connection to other, extra-terrestrial races that I submit are secretly and widely known to exist beyond our planet but are not yet openly recognised or officially acknowledged by any government or international authority.

The short reflective linking passage in the original book entitled *What is the Universe In?* was clearly at the heart of all this –as was the first story *Himself* in which the characters are all individual cells living inside one human body. I will confess now that I did not at the time of writing them fully understand what I was getting at with those two ideas.

I felt what I wrote very passionately, but was paradoxically shy of elaborating anything further. Making *What is the Universe In ?* the overall title of this new edition of the book is a deliberate choice which reflects my strong sense of certainty that my understanding has grown very significantly since then.

I will elaborate all these matters more fully in the new Postscript added at the end of the collection of stories. For the moment as we approach the original Prologue - the odd little poem *My Christmas List* inspired initially by the tiny gecko wall lizards with whom I often shared my imprisonment - I will hope and trust that readers old and new might enjoy the humour and irony of these curious stories from the void before pondering that final explanatory Postscript.

Norwich, England, Summer 2003

Prologue

A surrealistic Christmas dream of a man sealed off from the world, isolated, it seems, in time and space. All he has to give are the creations of his mind—products of doubtful value. But to whom? Nobody but himself.

> I'll get a gecko
> For El Greco
> And a lasso
> For Picasso
> Botticelli:
> Colour telly
> And this ash tray's
> For Velasquez.
>
> While for two pins
> For Reubens
> I'd get loo-bins
>
> For Van Gogh
> A Scottish loch
> For Van Dyke
> A Moulton bike
> And for Dali
> P'raps a Raleigh
> Plus for Goya
> A destroyer

PROLOGUE

I won't be stingy
There'll be conjee
For da Vinci.

For Cézanne
A Chinese fan
For Renoir
A Crunchie bar,
For Rembrandt
A potted plant
And for Gaugin
Whalebone probang

While to Constable
At luncheon
Give a truncheon

What for Gainsborough?
Give him Jane's bra!
To Raphael
La Tour Eiffel
To Matisse
A ten-year lease
With Monet
On Galway Bay

And to toothless
Canaletto
A false-setto

Man Alone

A man.
Sitting.
Alone.
Sitting alone for a long time.
Sitting alone for a long time in a room. A room which he may not leave. A room which has four walls, a floor and a ceiling. Six sides of a cube. A cube like a dice. Like a six-sided dice. And the man is sitting on a chair on the floor inside the cube. If it were a dice it would be a loaded dice, he feels. Loaded against him. Loaded by himself sitting on the floor of the dice, he feels. If it were picked up, thrown and rolled it would always land up the same way because the weight of the man is on the floor. And the side showing to the world outside would be the bland, featureless, bare upper side of the ceiling. Telling nothing. A kind of blank dice loaded against himself by himself. Loaded to, for, with, from and by himself, he feels.

The man is sitting alone for a very long time. A very, very long time. And because he is alone for a very long time with an empty mind he dreams.

With his eyes open. He dreams with his eyes open but always he returns to reality within the six-sided cube. After a very long time alone it is difficult for the man to know for certain whether or not he is losing his mind, going insane. He dreams with his eyes open, he dreams deliberately. But he always returns to the sickening reality of the six-sided cube. And for this he is grateful eventually. Because he comes to believe that insanity is the inability to wake up from dreaming with your eyes open. To remain sane in the six-sided cube he dreams desperately with his eyes open. But sometimes he fears that he may not be able to stop his open-eyed dreams. Perhaps the reality is that the insane dream all day with open eyes and never wake again. Perhaps they try to wake, but don't succeed.

But the need is compulsive and man must dream. He must walk the thin line between dream and finite reality. Perhaps fantasy is a way of assuring himself of his reality, by contrast. A distorting mirror which he holds up to himself and somehow illogically sees in it his reassuringly ordinary, earthbound image.

So drawing perverse comfort from his own physical inability to escape into the intangible world of unreality the man sitting alone for a long time, dreams.

He dreams of . . . himself.

Himself

Cell number 10047 closed the file he had been working on with a snap, placed it in the Supervisor's in-tray and said, with a hint of boredom in his voice: 'Estimated calcium requirements for maintaining hardness of 206 bones, 29 teeth and 20 toe and finger nails during the coming month, all present and correct, sir!'

The Supervisor of the Parathyroid Sub-Sections regarded the young cell for a moment and remarked mildly: 'I don't think there is any need for military overtones in the work of this department. And you might make a note that We may be losing one, if not two, teeth in the near future bringing the number down to 28 or possibly 27, thereby reducing future estimated needs.'

'Oh, have you heard something from Upstairs?' asked 10047 in the offhand manner he affected. 'Couple of Himself's molars dicky are they?'

The Supervisor, who thought the young cell's manner was bordering on impertinence, let a tinge of his disapproval show in the tone of his reply. 'It has been intimated to me from the Central Executive Offices that We are to have an inspection of the two teeth soon since they have been giving Us some trouble. Nothing further is certain at the moment. By the way, the deterioration is no reflection on the work of this department, I am told.'

The Supervisor allowed himself the indulgence of a smug smile. The older cell always used the royal or pontifical 'We' when referring to the organization in its entirety. In his young days terms such as 'Upstairs' and 'Himself' were unheard of. And no doubt these young upstarts had a whole range of such *dreadful* slang. His father before him, his grandfather before him and his grandfather's father before that had all supervised the Parathyroid Sub-Sections and the line stretched back to the Sub-Sections' very inception. It seemed to him that youngsters today weren't what they used to be. Didn't have the same sense of service in them.

The network of pipes, thick and thin, ducts and canals that ran past the Parathyroid Sub-Sections hummed and throbbed quietly but rhythmically with their usual morning efficiency. They looked for all the world like the complex pipe-lines of a giant chemical plant. There was an occasional gurgle from one of the ducts.

'Where would you say We are now,' asked 10047 of the Supervisor, idly. He thought perhaps his senior would be flattered by this appeal to his superior experience. Calm his ruffled feathers perhaps.

'In the 8.20 to Liverpool Street I would guess,'

replied the Supervisor after a moment. He cocked his head and listened to the sounds coming from outside the department. 'I should say We're quietly reading Our newspaper at present.' He coughed slightly, the way cells do, and pretended to busy himself with the cellular papers before him.

He wasn't going to show he was pleased at this unusual display of respect for his seniority from an underling. There was a long pause. It was quiet in the department this morning. The innumerable dials and gauges held steady on their norms. There was the usual subdued bustle in the back, the workshops section, as the delivery workers—10047 called them members of the Red Corps—unloaded their oxygen and other fuel and raw materials needed for the section's small-scale production and carted away the marketable calcium capsules, the carbon dioxide drums and other by-products for disposal. Everything was normal. There was no hint of the high drama to come later in the day.

'Exactly how old are We now?' asked 10047 trying to fight off the overpowering feeling of boredom that always came over him at this time each day.

'Established 1933. We have been in business now for a little over thirty-five years,' said the Supervisor. He was becoming a little suspicious of the young cell's innocent questions.

The unmistakable sound of half-a-dozen landing craft going by laden with armed troops came from an enclosed canal that ran close by.

'There go some more lads of the White Corps

off to the front to fight the foreign foe,' said 10047 lightly, after listening to them pass.

'Oh,' said the Supervisor raising his cellular eyebrows, 'since you seem so well-informed perhaps you might tell us where they are going—these "lads of the White Corps".' He liked white corpuscles to be called white corpuscles or at least white cells.

'I understand there's been a bit of trouble up on the nape of the neck these past few days,' said 10047 airily. 'Small invasion by foreign group. Nothing special. Usual sort of scrap. We lost a few but I think it's mostly cleared up by now. I fancy those boyos are going up more for mopping up than anything else. The White Corps' chief is in a bit of a flap apparently. Just when he wanted all the air he could get to help him seal off the area, Himself apparently goes and bangs a plaster on the outside —what He calls a small boil—completely gumming up the works. The Chief's been on to Upstairs about it and they hope to get Himself to tear it off later today. But they don't promise anything. You know what they are, "we can only recommend and advise".' 10047 mimicked the last phrase in a bureaucratic voice.

Then he noticed with a sudden pang of unease that the Supervisor was regarding him with unusual intentness. In his desire to show off his knowledge of affairs, had he perhaps been indiscreet?

'Tell me just exactly how you know all that,' said the Supervisor, speaking very quietly.

'Um, well,' 10047 hesitated and flushed slightly

as cells are wont to do. 'I've, . . . um, I've got a pal in one of the departments Upstairs,' he said finally, not knowing how this would be received.

'And how exactly do you get in touch with him since you never leave this department?'

10047 glanced round at the little desk instruments in the department, the terminals of the vast Communications Network. He listened to the soft hum from the trunk lines outside as messages whizzed back and forth between the Central Executive Offices and all departments at speeds of around 300 m.p.h. His gaze rested for a moment on the junction boxes marked Sensory System, Voluntary Motor System and Autonomic System. He took a deep breath and said, with a rush, 'Well, we sometimes have a chat through the old Communications Network—only in the absolutely quiet times when there's no other traffic,' he added hastily, realizing his chief was likely to be displeased.

'I hardly need to remind you,' said the Supervisor severely, 'of the seriousness of misusing the Communications.' But he didn't say more. He was secretly impressed by his subordinate's contact and already realized it might be of help to him some time in short-circuiting normal channels.

'Who is your "pal"?' he asked at length, a slight sarcastic inflection on the last word.

'B.C. 1474729,' replied the young cell using the 'B.C.' prefix enviously. If there ever came a chance he would dearly love to become a B.C. (Brain Cell). All the others were entitled to the L.C. (Living

Cell) prefix but nobody ever used it since it was so common.

The Supervisor, remembering he should be reproving, cut sharply into the L.C.'s thoughts.

'Have you no work to do, 10047?'

'Well, nothing that isn't absolutely routine and rather dull,' the young cell replied, surprised at his own boldness, 'and rather than spread it thinly over the day I can pack it all away in half an hour later on.'

The Supervisor raised his cellular eyebrows again but said nothing. He imagined this look combined majestic aloofness, imperious disdain and dignified apartness appropriate in a departmental head.

'What I mean is,' said 10047 deciding to crash on, 'the work here isn't very exciting, is it? Now if I was down in Adrenals it would be different. Just imagine! Life being concerned solely with danger and excitement. Waiting at the ready to shovel out a lashing of the precious adrenalin into the jolly old network. Then sitting back and watching the old pipe-lines constrict, all the pressure gauges going up, the whole works throbbing at a new faster level, going flat out, key pitch, bang, bang, bang!'

He stopped and looked at the Supervisor. Perhaps wouldn't do to get too carried away.

'Your work here is equally important, if less spectacular,' the older cell said with a firm note of censure. 'And perhaps there's one thing you haven't considered, our far superior position. We are pleasantly situated adjoining Thyroid Departments in a high frontal position that is eminently desirable. Adrenals Division, of which you seem inordinately fond, on the other hand have their two sections well down in the,' he paused and a note of distaste crept into his voice, 'in the lumbar region, directly adjoining the Decontamination and Filter Plants at Area Kidney.'

10047 made no reply to this. How typical that the old celliferous fool should think only about their position on the map rather than what they did!

'Of course,' said 10047, letting his voice go a little dreamy, as cells can, 'if ever there came a chance to remuster, which I know is without precedent, I should really like to go Upstairs.' He paused reflectively, then continued even more dreamily: 'Pituitary Control . . .' He let the words roll deliciously off his tongue. 'Pituitary Control, what Himself would call the master gland. Send a team of hormones here, send a team of hormones there and all the L.C.s behind the doors marked Thyroid Department, Parathyroid Sub-Section, Pancreas, Adrenals Divisions and the others jump to your commands. Position, influence, respect! Or even to move into the rarefied atmosphere of the Central Executive Offices themselves. The grey, computerized complex corridors of power! Cranium House! The Whitehall of our world! . . .' He stopped suddenly and looked up. 'Hello, what's happening to the old plumbing?'

The steady quiet rhythm in the pipe-lines had suddenly increased. The lights in the department were burning brighter. There was an up-tempo pounding from the whole network. Everybody in the department instinctively turned expectant eyes to the automatic warning board. But the red Emergency sign didn't come on, nor did the 'Action Stations' hooter sound. After a few moments the rhythm began to slow and soon returned to normal.

'Well,' said 10047, letting out a long breath, 'talking of the boys in Adrenals, that was clearly their doing! Wonder what it was. Didn't last long anyway did it? Perhaps someone fired off by mistake. I shall have to ask my pal Upstairs.'

Somewhere far below the Parathyroid Sub-Sections, the Fuel Refinery and Processing Division and its several satellite Construction and Maintenance Units had already begun work on a new consignment of raw materials that had recently arrived. Refinery's Chief Engineer was on the line to somebody on high in Central Executive.

'How do you find today's first delivery, Chief?' the B.C. was saying. 'We had more time than usual today to think of you.'

'Fine, just fine—in itself,' the chief added with that note of reserve that every good N.C.O. knew indicated respectfully to the officer and gentleman with whom he was dealing that things were not quite as they might be. He waited for his cue so that the officer and gentleman could think later that his astute perception uncovered the problem.

'Something's bothering you, Chief, I divine,' said the voice of the B.C. on the line, taking up the bait nicely.

'Well, sir, we're all very pleased to see bacon, coffee, eggs, butter and so on back in the consignment today. It's some time since we've seen that, sir. We'd begun to get accustomed to much less and even no morning delivery at all on occasions.'

'Well Chief,' the finely modulated tones of the B.C. broke in. 'You know how it is. We are a frantically busy up-and-coming bachelor business executive who does things in a hurry, works late, sleeps little.' He laughed the little laugh of a superior confiding in a subordinate.

'That's as may be, sir, but with due respect,'— the chief had decided to presist—'with due respect, it's not going to be good enough. You know, sir, as well as I that it's not only the morning delivery that has been a bit haphazard. Two large measures of whisky and a very small quantity of bread, butter and ham at midday, hurriedly consigned, does not make the most of the processing equipment at Our disposal. To coin a phrase, sir, it's under-employed.'

The B.C. began to interrupt.

'Ah, I know what you're going to say sir. It's made up for later, often with a very heavy consignment late in the evening. Quite right. But you know, it's the wrong time and once again with due respect, doesn't always help us in richness ratios. Overall, sir, we've dipped fairly heavily into the glucose reserves held at Liver Pool. They're almost out there. The next thing we'll have to go over to fats conversion with according weight loss. And my people dealing with alcohol are rarely under-employed,' he added in a matter-of-fact voice. Then he continued in what he hoped might be construed as an ominous tone by his listener. 'I'm having my maintenance chaps keep a very careful daily eye on the Duodenum Section of the pipe-line—regular inspections—for signs of construction stress, material fatigue—we can't be too careful on Duodenal faults. What we should like down here is regular balanced deliveries three times daily, sir. It's in Our best interests.'

'O.K. Chief, I'll do what I can. But you know the position up here. We don't have the final decision on these things . . .' The Chief Engineer, raising his cellular eyes heavenwards chanted under his breath in unison with the B.C. the final inevitable phrase . . . 'We can only recommend and advise.'

He hung up and went back to his work shaking his head in that peculiar way cells have.

Upstairs the B.C. put down his instrument and remarked to a colleague with a laugh: 'Chiefy's carping about irregularity of supplies again. I suppose we'd better have another go at it.'

He drew a memo pad towards him and began to write. His printed heading was addressed to 'I' who was, they knew not what exactly, and who dwelt, they knew not where. They were not even sure where the memos they composed eventually arrived. They were whisked away on the internal postal system and disappeared forever in the maze of the grey corridors. They could indeed only advise and recommend to the attention of the mysterious, omnipresent, omnipotent, yet evanescent 'I'.

Back in the Parathyroid Sub-Sections L.C. 10047 had just finished making a quick and very discreet call indeed to his 'pal' Upstairs.

'Well, well, well,' he said slowly and a little tantalizingly as he knew the Supervisor was eagerly waiting for the news, 'that *is* interesting.' He wore a broad celluliferous grin.

'Know what the cause of all the excitement was?' he asked, addressing the Supervisor and all the other expectant L.C.s in the department. Obviously they didn't and after one or two had chorused rather testily, 'No, no, what was it?' 10047 deigned to let them in on the somewhat spicy secret.

'New secretary!' he said smugly. 'What we were treated to was the reaction of Himself to the first sight of his new secretary on arrival at the office. According to information received from the two Observation Outlets in the mighty Optics Unit her L.C.s are really stacked, lads, really stacked! A regular dish of the most succulent variety I am told. Judging from what we noticed here I should think it was a case of lust at first sight!'

There was a little buzz of discussion at this.

Half aloud, half to himself, 10047 mused on the topic. 'Just imagine, a fine, gently undulating, soft, fragrant, warm, splendidly-stacked assemblage of feminine L.C.s. Wouldn't mind getting involved with something in that direction myself.' He had been gazing dreamily into the middle distance. As he focussed again he realized the Supervisor had been listening. 'Of course,' he continued, 'if there was to be any chance of that I'd have to change direction in my remustering intentions, wouldn't I? It wouldn't be a matter of "going up!" but of "going down!" Have to get myself a slot in the Glamour Department wouldn't I?'

The Supervisor lost his breath at this. He tried to cough to hide it, choked, spluttered and went red in his cellular face. Only after several minutes was he able to speak again.

'If by the Glamour Department you mean the Reproduction Unit I suggest you use its correct term.' He turned away abruptly but to his own surprise found he was having to suppress a smile at the unconventional nomenclature employed by the young 10047.

In the early evening 10047 announced gleefully to his Parathyroid Sub-Section colleagues that Herself was to be taken to dinner that evening—for so, had he already dubbed the new secretary who had made such an impressive impact earlier in the day. 10047 had picked up this latest intelligence from another surreptitious chat with his B.C. friend.

By 9.30 p.m. Refinery and Processing's disgruntled chief was aware that it was likely to be something of a gala night in his Division. What was clearly going to be a long and steady consignment of a wide variety had begun. The wines and spirits range was already impressive. In addition to the familiar Scotch spirit early on there had been an aperitif and two kinds of wine had just been sent down. Chiefy had already predicted publicly to his subordinates they would see champagne arrive as well before the night was out. There had been a wide selection of hors d'oeuvres, a very good and useful turtle soup with sherry which had clearly been set afire in a thimble-sized ladle immediately before the union. Now there was smoked salmon and daintily-sliced brown bread. The Division was settling down under the chief's eye to a long spell of overtime again tonight.

The chief took a call from Central Executive. It was the same B.C. he had spoken to earlier.

'Well Chief, trust you're happy with what we're doing for you tonight,' he said very jovially.

'Aye, sir. There's some good quality raw material arriving right enough,' replied the chief in his taciturn way.

'There'll be plenty more yet, Chief, plenty more, before the night's out. Roast pheasant, cranberry sauce, game chips . . .' He reeled off a string of commodities half of which the chief couldn't catch. There was something a little odd about the B.C., he thought. '. . . crêpe suzettes or possibly strawberries and cream'—he was still going on—'and champagne to finish it!' he concluded breathlessly.

'Aye, I thought that would be it, sir,' said the chief. 'Very good then, sir, if there's nothing else I'll be getting back to my work.'

'No, that's all. Oh about that other thing earlier today. I've written a memo. Can't do more can we?' The B.C. laughed loudly. 'Well, keep up the good work, Chief,' he added flippantly and went off.

The chief puzzled over the B.C.'s unusually erratic behaviour as he went back to work. If he hadn't known it was too early to be possible, he would have said it was a case of inebriation. At last he gave it up. Of course the chief had no way of knowing that the first heady moments of love and infatuation with a beautiful girl can sometimes produce an effect that is very similar to intoxication. All the B.C.s tonight found themselves unaccountably bright and frivolous, found themselves being terribly clever and on form—and sometimes even a bit silly too!

Much later L.C. 10047, fresh from a call Upstairs, gave a progress report to his gossip-hungry colleagues. 'Seems Our dinner was a roaring success. We seem to be making a big impression with Herself. We were right at the top of Our wits tonight. Oh my word We were funny and amusing and charming and everything rolled into one.' 10047 struck a few exaggerated cellular attitudes to illustrate his report in what he imagined was a satirical vein.

'We are at present at Herself's apartment for a

nightcap having gallantly escorted Her home and We are now, if you please,'—he rolled his eyes heavenwards—'playing with Herself's pet kitten. Or should I say trying to, since the creature has apparently contrived to get itself out of the window and is crouching on a narrow ledge outside refusing to budge. The apartment I might add is twelve storeys up in a fashionable part of London. At the time of my call Upstairs, Himself, to the considerable amusement of a lot of B.C.s, was leaning out of the window endeavouring to entice the creature in, watched by the anxious but adoring Herself.'

Further ironic comment from 10047 was suddenly stifled by an abrupt step-up in the tempo of activity in the surrounding pipe-lines. The lights brightened to a new intensity and the L.C.s of Parathyroid Sub-Sections waited expectantly to see what the development meant. The level of activity held at about that noticed earlier in the day, perhaps slightly higher.

'Well,' said 10047 reflectively after a pause, 'I should think there could be two explanations. Either We have already rescued the kitten and are being suitably rewarded by Herself, or We are attempting something heroically risky and impressive in order to do same.'

The Supervisor, his voice very serious, broke in. 'I think you can forget about your first guess, 10047. Experience has taught me to distinguish roughly between stimuli for accelerated employment of all capacities. I think We are committed to a possibly dangerous situation.'

There was a tense silence. Slowly but unmistakably the tempo was increasing. Pipe-lines were constricting, pressure gauges showed increased readings.

It seemed certain to the waiting L.C.s that They were out on the narrow ledge twelve storeys high over London, crawling along it to reach the kitten. All eyes were fixed on the automatic warning board to see if the situation would develop into an ultimate state of emergency.

'I suppose,' breathed 10047, his cellular face set in unusually grim lines, 'the only way Himself could possibly know how us L.C.s feel in such situations would be for him to be in a submarine in some kind of difficulty.' Nobody replied. Tension was rising with the tempo of what was now clearly danger mobilization of resources.

Although they had been aware of the possibility of it sounding, the raucous and repeated rasp of the Action Stations hooter startled them when it came. The red Emergency sign blazed on. Lighting reached full intensity. With hardly a sign from the Supervisor the Sub-Sections staff slipped smoothly into their assigned roles. The Sub-Section shut down its supply intakes to absolute minimum since it had no active part to play in the emergency.

Its role, like many of the units in the organization, was one of minimum interference. But Adrenals Division was working flat out. It was feeding in large quantities of its rich fuel. Pressure gauges showed that maximum pressure was now obtaining. Pipe-line constriction was also maximum and the pumping rate had trebled. The pounding throb of maximum mobilization gripped the entire organization.

The L.C.s of Parathyroid Sub-Sections waited, keyed up and on edge—most of them had never experienced anything as serious as this before. Then the Sixth Sense wall tannoy, rarely ever used, crackled into life. The L.C.s held their breaths. It was 'I' making a direct announcement to all points.

'The situation is extremely serious,' the authoritative voice said. It was not difficult to detect the edge of high tension in it either. But 'I' did not gabble the announcement despite the extreme nature of the emergency.

'At present We are hanging by Our fingertips from a ledge twelve storeys up with solid concrete pavement far below. We almost fell while crawling on the ledge but managed to make a grab to assume the present very difficult position. I want all to make the greatest possible effort to contribute to the attempt to hang on until help arrives.

'I need hardly say what the consequences of failure to do so will be. I know most of you run yourselves, in effect, most of the time, quite independently of anything I might do, but this is one occasion when a supreme effort is required or there will be no question of running yourselves in the future. You know what I mean . . . Thank you everybody.'

The tannoy crackled and went silent. The tension had become almost unbearable. The moments ticked by. The L.C.s knowing their fate hung in the balance quite literally, were silent, motionless. All energy and power was concentrated on the vital Extremity Areas involved in the survival task of holding on.

The Supervisor did, however, whisper briefly to 10047. 'See now the importance of your work. The strength of some of your well-maintained 206 bones is now contributing a vital part to this endurance.'

10047 nodded respectfully, looking drawn and serious.

Moments stretched into minutes. The Emergency indicator still blazed out. The pounding tempo did not slacken. Surely this mighty effort could not be sustained much longer in such adverse conditions. Suddenly there was a great lurch and an entirely new and terrifying sensation was felt. Plunging, falling, the Sub-Section seemed to turn end over end. The lights seemed to whirl and swim above, then below. Down, down, plummeting down, long and slow and awful.

Then another more terrifying, lurching, shuddering impact. Now it seemed there was a sensation of rising, shooting upwards but faster than in any lift. Then down once again, much shorter this time and another bone-shaking, breathtaking impact. A tumbling sensation—and They were at rest. The L.C.s who had endured this gripped with terror looked uncomprehendingly about them. The lights were still on at full brightness. That seemed to be favourable. The emergency rhythm continued. But just as they began to breathe sighs of relief, the lights flickered and dimmed abruptly to an eerie blue glow. They all looked anxiously to the Supervisor in the strange gloom for an explanation.

'I think I'm right in saying,' he said almost in a whisper, 'that We've fainted.' He peered through the strange light. 'This is not the deep indigo that one remembers experiencing on sudden devastating departures from consciousness on the rugger field. At the risk of being unduly optimistic I would say—following that terrible and quite unprecedented falling sensation—that some kind of soft impact was achieved. We must await patiently full details of its outcome and damage, if any.'

At that moment lights flickered up again to a dim working level. Along the Para-Sympathetic lines of communication messages were buzzing, bringing the racing machinery back to its normal, even, subdued rhythm.

10047 itched to get on to his pal Upstairs but knew that in this post-crisis period it was quite impossible. He would have to wait patiently until the morning. He didn't know it now but then he would discover and announce to the eagerly receptive L.C.s of his department that they were in hospital. Just for observation, you know. No serious damage. Few bruises that was all. Be out in a few days at the most. Himself had suffered a bit of shock. Had clung on to the ledge by his fingertips for nearly ten minutes. By then the fire brigade had rushed to the scene and got one of their jumping things ready down below—you know the things suitable for plunging into from great heights in burning buildings. It had been a rather good effort all round actually, 10047 would find himself saying. Good, solid, dependable bone construction had played a big part. Lot of important work to be done in these Sub-Sections. Of course L.C. 10047 wouldn't realize it, but he himself would be suffering a bit from shock for a few days too.

The Chief Engineer of Fuel Refinery and Processing Division didn't yet know either that he would be pleased with the coming few days. Quiet, very regular consignments of supplies. No trouble with richness ratios since all that was nicely balanced and worked out by experts in that sort of thing. And in the near future the chief would become even more pleased when he learned of the merger of the entire Organization with another— dubbed by 10047 as Herself. One result of this merger would be that the part of the business with which the chief was concerned would benefit greatly under the new management and good regular consignments of supplies would become an everyday occurence. When he finally learned of this the chief would grin that slow grin of satisfaction—the one that cells do so engagingly.

What is the Universe In?

Left alone for an eternal long time the mind of the man begins to conceive the very strangeness of reality. Wage packets and mortgages, tube trains and buses, jobs and homes, families and wives and friends and enemies are as nothing. Left alone for a long time the most overpowering and frightening question is: what is the universe in? When looking at the blank wall of the six-sided cube for a long time and after a lot of thought, the man is often on the brink of the answer. He feels that suddenly he is about to become aware of the total reality. It's on the tip of his tongue. Total understanding is standing at his elbow, and sometimes moves even closer. But close as the final explanation comes—closer than it ever came before or was ever after to come—it eludes the firmness of his grasp. Nevertheless the hint remains. The universe *is* in *something*. All life must be relative. The ant hill, the teeming capital city, the bacilli in a head of pus are of a relation, are of a progression.

One day far ahead when man is woman too in one body he will walk to the top of a hill in the dawn, thoroughly complete, and everything a million years old will explode in a shower of light. Perhaps some unimaginably gargantuan figure in which the universe resides unseen will say to his equally gargantuan wife: 'Ouch. That pain in my toe for the past few days got worse just then, but now it seems to have disappeared completely.'

Oppressed by such thoughts the man, of terrifying smallness and insignificance, dreams his wide-awake dreams. It seems his dreams are the only things that give him stature. So he dreams a mundane dream of leaves, of an old man and leaves.

The Old Man
and the Leaves

The pale, clear sunshine of a late autumn afternoon shone down on the little park in the centre of the city. Birds that wheeled in the bright sky above, looking down, could see through the branches of the trees, fast becoming bare of their leaves, the figure of an old man sweeping the paths of the park with a brush made of twigs. As he worked sharp gusts of wind snatched more dying leaves from the trees and sent them dashing in the air around him in a blizzard of bronze and gold. As fast as he swept and shovelled into his barrow fresh leaves settled behind him again like naughty children. But he worked on steadily.

In the little park the noise of the traffic and of the city all around was subdued. People going to offices and factories in the morning or returning to catch buses and trains home in the evening liked to walk through its quiet tree-lined paths, among its neat flower beds. They brought their sandwiches and sat on the benches to eat them when it was fine at lunchtime. The old man always had a cheerful word to exchange with them as he went about his jobs.

As the smoky dusk of autumn fell that afternoon he trundled the last load of leaves back to the enclosure behind his cottage in the corner of the park, went round and locked up the four gates and returned to the little cottage where he lived alone.

The cottage was close by a small group of swings, a roundabout and a slide. He liked to hear the excited cries of the children when they played there during the day. In the garden behind the cottage vegetables grew fat and round under his care. The flowers in the beds of the park bloomed fuller and brighter than in any other park in the city. 'If anybody has got green fingers, he has,' the Parks Superintendent, who visited from time to time, would say.

The old man had lived and worked in the little park in the centre of the city for as long as anyone could remember. Some of the older people who went often through the park thought they could recall his being there when they were very young. His face, gnarled by the years and tanned deep by the weathers, was itself now like a wrinkled leaf of autumn. Some fancied they saw him talking to the trees sometimes; especially that great oak tree that stood by the hedge near the main gate. They imagined that must be his favourite tree. They were right, it was. And he did talk to the trees. They never answered him of course, but he went on talking to them and would sometimes give one an affectionate slap with his hand as he worked the ground around it. To the old man the oaks, elms and silver birch, the beech trees, the plane trees and the horse chestnuts were strong, quiet friends. He watched them every day in their different moods. He watched them in the fierce winds when they flailed their branches angrily like a woman constantly clutching at a hat that threatened to blow away. He watched them in the quiet rain when they rejoiced in the patter of the drops on their leaves. He watched them in the fog when they stood black, dripping and wary; in the dark when they rustled gently in repose; in the dawn when they stirred with the breeze to welcome the day. He watched them in the warm sun when they smiled and relaxed and drank in the warmth and light. He watched them grow each year. The little park in the centre of the city was like an oasis of grass and earth and trees free to breathe and grow in the middle of the desert of concrete and tarmacadam that overlaid and stifled the barren land all around. He watched the trees grow in this oasis and in his mind he likened the leaves of the trees to the people of the city.

Most people that came to the park only really noticed the trees when they blossomed in the spring and when they shed their leaves in profusion in the autumn; the beauty of childhood, the finality of agedness. But the old man saw the tiny barely-formed leaves that fell in the early spring before they had hardly taken a hold on life. Later he saw others which, when growing quickly and well, inexplicably changed from green to brilliant yellow, their vitality mysteriously gone and they fluttered to the ground before the best days of summer had arrived. He saw those rich healthy leaves torn bodily from the trees in high winds and flung down on the paths, perhaps a whole family on a sturdy twig, cut off from the living tree in the full bloom of life. But the ripe foliage as a body lived on and the trees always looked the same to a casual visitor. As the summer ended and autumn wore on the leaves detached themselves in turn. Some, the old man thought sometimes, seemed eager to be gone when the days were yet warm. Many whirled away when the cold winds began to blow hard. Others hung on and battled with the gales and rain for days before joining their fellows in the thick carpet below. A few clung to their trees with a fierce tenacity until they stood out alone on the bare black branches and only very reluctantly did they finally forsake life when the threat of snow was in the air.

The next morning the old man rose before the sun as always, opened the gates of the little park in the centre of the city and began his work again. He had been sweeping the leaves for many days and was surprised to find himself uncommonly tired by the task. Most of the leaves had fallen now and lay in deep copper-coloured troughs at the sides of the avenues and at the hedge bottoms. Small boys ran delightedly knee-deep through them, throwing armfuls in the air and shrieking

THE OLD MAN AND THE LEAVES

with the fun of it. As he worked round by the main gate the old man noticed that the oak tree, his favourite, was bare—well almost. A solitary leaf, large for the oak, clung on firmly in the morning wind, swaying on a branch jutting out over the pathway. He stood looking up at it for a moment then went quickly on sweeping with his brush of twigs.

That afternoon the Parks Superintendent made one of his rare visits to the little park in the centre of the city. He knew everything would be in order but he liked to have a chat with the old man from time to time. 'You've got your work cut out this year by the look of things,' he said, glancing round the leaf-cluttered paths. The old man stopped and laid aside his brush and shovel. 'Aye, there's a lot of leaves this year. More'n usual. Been a lovely summer.' He lit his pipe and puffed ruminatively at it.

'Sure you can manage it all right on your own?' said the Parks Superintendent, thinking the old man looked more tired than in other years.

'I don't promise you I'll sweep up every leaf in the park,' he said, a twinkle in his faded blue eyes. When he grinned the countless lines of age in his nut-brown face deepened, crossed and counter-crossed until he looked like some mischievous woodland deity who had lived a thousand years. 'Same as yer might say that no matter how long a man might study books all his days, he'll never know everything. Or no matter how hard we try, we can't cure all the ills of the world once and for all. But I reckon I'll manage to get as much done as'll make the park look neat as it ever did.'

The Parks Superintendent grinned and gave him a friendly pat on the shoulder. 'Good. Just wondered if you needed any help.' He looked up at the skies greying over in the fading light and at the dark, gaunt branches of the trees. 'Always makes me feel a bit sad, the autumn,' he said to the old man. 'You know, the end of the greenness and the growing and the cold hard winter to come.'

The old man gazed around thoughtfully through the slow curl of his pipe smoke before replying. 'Aye, but don't forget, although things look as though they've come to a standstill and everything's dead, the end of one growing season is just the start of another. Nature never really stops for a minute. She's making preparations right now, you can bet, to dazzle us again next spring.'

The Parks Superintendent laughed. 'I suppose you're right as always. By the way,' he added, 'how old are you now?'

'I'm over eighty,' replied the old man. He knocked out his pipe, picked up his brush and with another wrinkled grin at the Parks Superintendent resumed his sweeping.

'Well, mind you take good care of yourself,' said the younger man, and he got on his bicycle and rode away. Funny thing he thought as he pedalled on home, ever since he could remember first asking the old man his age his reply had always been the same 'Over eighty'.

For the next few days the old man worked unsparingly from dawn to dusk at his task of clearing the leaves from the little park in the centre of the city. Autumn was turning to winter now and all the trees were bare at last. Well, all except one that is —the big oak tree by the main gate. There the single stubborn leaf remained, despite the efforts of the wind and rain to tear it free. Each day the old man paused to gaze at it for a while, then carried on sweeping and shovelling, sweeping and shovelling. The mound of leaves in the enclosure behind the cottage had grown to an enormous size. He carried on doggedly despite his growing weariness and early one afternoon in mid-December he carted the last barrow-load to the enclosure. He stacked away the brush made of twigs, the shovel and the barrow and gazed with satisfaction around the neat avenues and gardens. It had been hard, long toil but it was done now! Lighting his pipe he plodded slowly and thoughtfully across to the main gate. The little park in the centre of the city was still and deserted that afternoon and as he walked he gloried in its quiet beauty. Beneath the old oak tree he stopped and looked up at the one big leaf that had refused to fall. 'So you're still there then, old friend,' he said softly. He gazed at it for long moments, his

faded blue eyes unwavering. He thought perhaps
he saw it begin to droop a little or was he imagining it? He lowered his tired old body on to the
bench beneath the tree and smoked his pipe contentedly now his work was finished. The park
around him was gentle and calm as if it sought to
soothe the old man. He lifted his tired eyes again
to look at the leaf. He was feeling very, very weary
now. And this time he was sure he saw it droop a
little on the twig. The hand holding the pipe fell
gently to his side and he placed it on the bench beside him. His eyelids felt heavy and drowsiness
overcame him. His eyes closed and his chin sank
forward a little on his chest. The park around him
was silent.

Without a sound the oak leaf on the tree above
detached itself from the branch and floated gently
down, spinning in the still air until it lighted softly
in the old man's lap. It was a big copper-coloured
leaf of unusual beauty, finely veined, wrinkled and
subtly hued. A light breeze sprang up and the few
remaining leaves that nested in the short grass and
at the roots of the hedges whisked and danced across
the ground, swirled around the bench where the
old man sat and clustered against his boots. Then
suddenly a great strong wind was blowing hard
from the other side of the park! It tore great flurries
of leaves from the enclosure behind the old man's
cottage and sent them racing and tumbling in their
thousands towards the bench under the oak tree.
When it ceased a flame and saffron-coloured mound

of leaves was piled high around the oak, completely engulfing the bench beneath it. For a few moments all was still again in the little park in the centre of the city.

Then once more the great wind blew. In one sweep it picked up the mound of leaves as though in a mighty fist and flung them furiously in the air. They spun and soared high in the afternoon sky. They scattered far over the hedges of the park. They blew among the factory chimneys and the tall office buildings in great clouds. People began looking up surprised to see such a sudden commotion of leaves in the wind. They blew away in all directions drifting to the fields and on beyond to the sea. In the little park in the centre of the city the bench under the oak tree where the old man had been sitting was empty. Even the pipe that rested there had gone.

As the afternoon wore on a mother brought her small boy to the little park in the centre of the city. She sat in one of the shelters and let him romp on the grass before her. Fair-haired with wide blue eyes he was still unsteady on his short legs and was just learning to talk. He gambolled back and forth, sometimes tumbling, sometimes stopping to stare with innocent wonder at a blade of grass or a bird. He trotted beneath the oak tree, picked up something and ran back to his mother. He held out a hand to show her. 'Yes darling, that's a leaf,' she said, looking at the big copper-coloured oak leaf, that he held. *It* was unusually beautiful, finely veined, wrinkled and subtly hued. 'Leaf!' he repeated slowly. 'Leaf.' Then off he darted waving it above his head in one small hand. Suddenly the wind whisked it from him under the oak tree itself. He stood still, his little head thrown back, staring upwards open-mouthed as the oak leaf sailed and soared up and away and disappeared in the wind.

Still looking up at the oak tree his sharp young eyes caught sight of something else. He looked to his mother sitting some distance away and pointing upwards with a tiny arm he shouted ' 'Nother leaf!' His mother smiled. She could see nothing in the gathering dusk but the dark empty branches. She thought fondly that her son was just showing off the new word he had learned. But he was right. There was one tiny new young green leaf growing on the tree although it was cold December.

Prayers Whispered into a Bath

Often the man was overwhelmed by his own helplessness to free himself. Equally often he was overwhelmed by the failure of his fellows to help him. And he was overwhelmed too by the intimidating closeness of the warders who had no wish to help him. At these frequent times he withdrew. He withdrew into his own mind and he withdrew into darkness. The man went into the washroom and closed the door at night. He turned out the light. He was as far as he could be from his warders. In the pitch-black darkness he asked for freedom. Perhaps the darkness was the nearest he could get to oblivion in which he might become a disembodied mind in which the pain of confinement might be eased. The man knelt at the side of the bath and said prayers. And at first he was startled by the sound of his whispered prayers echoing back at him from the bath. The smooth, white, elongated bowl of the bath which was only a faint paleness in the gloom turned the words gently back to him. Soon the sounds of his own whispered prayers for freedom coming back to him out of the bath became a comfort. In the darkness the bath whispered the words of the Lord's Prayer with him. It became a place to retreat to. Like a church where the sounds of their own prayers have comforted countless people.

In winter when the bare branches of the tree outside the window were jagged black scratches on the grey slate surface of the sky three birds came every day at five o'clock as the light was fading. They chirped and twittered in the branches and twigs of the tree. The man sitting alone watched them. And the warders watched them. They saw that one of the birds was ruffle-feathered. An ordinary grey sparrow but with ruffled feathers always about the neck. It gave her an unkempt, slapdash air. But the other, smoother birds pursued her endlessly. Chirping and twittering from twig to twig. The bright-eyed bird with the ruffled feathers played hard to get and jumped around, staring apparently unseeing into the distance. And the other two danced shameless attendance on her. The man watched and the warders watched. Their retinas recorded the same images in the fading grey light. But they watched separately and nowhere was there a meeting or joining between them. The birds came every day at five as if they had tiny time-pieces built into their consciousness. Immediately afterwards they must have roosted for the night. The man in the six-sided cube came to expect them in the quiet yard. And the warders came to expect them too. But they watched them separately and apart.

In spring the tree in the yard ceased to stand black and gaunt outside the window. Suddenly it was as if a mist of green specks hovered around the fine fingers of the twigs in the tree. In the cracks between the stones of the yard minute pinheads of green also appeared. The eyes of the man, idle and underemployed, picked out these things that would have been invisible to a busy man. Each day the flecks of green underfoot and overhead grew until they were visible to all. And against all reason the renewal of life was an encouragement to the man alone. These incomprehensible atoms of life fed the hope in the man although nothing ever happened to confirm it.

In the warmth of the summer the clear light of the early evening sun shone on the tree. In full leaf and rich with white blossom the tree stood in the evening light. For a time the man was transfixed by the sight. It took on the aura of a vision in the isolated mind of the man. And the leaves and the blossom in the pale sunlight were the goodness of life. There was a basic goodness in life, itself a powerful force. And the man knew it would be all right. If he was ever to see a vision this was it. The clear yellow light of the sun on the green leaves and white blossom of a tree.

THE OLD MAN AND THE LEAVES

Closely confined alone the man dreamed himself out of his confining walls. Dreamed himself far away amongst trees, grass and flowers. And his dream brought him within touching distance, too of . . . Well, to cut a long story short . . .

To Cut a Long
Story Short ...

The warm spring rain tapped gently at the window of his apartment. Blown by a mild, friendly wind, the large droplets that were already drenching the roof-tops of London and causing people to scurry in the streets below, beckoned him from his book with their insistent patter on the glass. He rose, walked to the window and looked out.

The glistening hiss of rain has a quiet beauty. Today, falling with heavy voluptuous splashes on the sill it was vibrant and seductive and drew him out in coat and hat. He made for the park.

London's parks, quiet oases in the motorized roar of the surrounding desert, are at their best by rain. He often went to the park when it rained for then most people shunned and sheltered, dashed for taxis and buses, put their heads down and their collars up and ceased looking at each other and the world.

He walked with his head up in the rain. It lanced down into wide black puddles around his feet on the quiet deserted pathways. Tiny crystal pyramids leapt up, shimmered and fell back as the invasion built up its strength in the puddles. Countless evanescent rings spreading into and through each other announced the arrival of each new puncture. Bubbles sprang into being at the force of the heavier plops, eddied and circled around for a moment, burst and were gone to be replaced by others. Like people on the world.

He walked on, this tallish, youngish man in a hat and coat, the rain that had invited him out blowing softly against his face. The green park, the rain and the quiet were his. At first he was only vaguely aware that he was sharing it. Then because his longer stride gradually overhauled her shorter one, he saw the girl on the path in front of him. Sometimes trailing a hand through the leaves of a bush that shone heavy with the silver rain. For a moment he knew that quickening which the first sight of a beautiful woman invokes in a man. She wore a silk square of green and gold over her hair, a drab beige raincoat belted tightly with a twisted belt and almost mannish suede shoes with flat heels and laces at the front. But without seeing her face he knew she would be beautiful. A beautiful woman declares herself wordlessly. Something unmistakable is emanated. Beauty perhaps is a force in its own right that is not to be denied. And beauty moves beautifully.

Walking behind her he noticed that faint splashes from the puddles marked the backs of her bare legs. Her ankles were slim but strong-looking. Her calves were rounded, tapering, sunburned. She

A MAN ALONE

was slender but not as the rangy clothes-horse fashion model is slender. The swell and curve of her hips under the tightly-belted raincoat drew his eyes with the fascination of their movement as she walked, almost indolently, in the rain—a movement which has drawn the eyes of man across the centuries.

One of the few Latin quotations he had bothered to commit to memory—perhaps because of its sensual connotation—came to him now. *Vera incessu patuit dea*—by her gait the true goddess is revealed.

And the goddess walked on through the rain in the London park.

She was alone but not lonely. Some people when alone radiate silent distress signals in their isolation. But she was alone by choice, at ease and complete. He suddenly had the seemingly absurd notion that this was a moment of great importance. Perhaps their paths had crossed to be joined. This might be the beginning of the story of life with this beautiful girl. Perhaps this was his wife. He smiled at this unfamiliar thought. He, a bachelor who drank deeply and satisfyingly from the heady cup of successful bachelorhood.

He had slowed his pace to remain behind her and smiled again now through the rain as he wondered what she would think of his thoughts as he drank in the movement of her hips before him. The hem of the raincoat stopped the eyes at the back of the knees. From then on it was fanciful conjecture.

But perhaps women would not be so shocked and horrified if they knew the thoughts of men. Polite society probably credited woman with too much naiveté about her impact. It was a pretence, furthered by the niceties of conversation, that created the gulf between thought and word.

Grinning to himself and thinking these thoughts of the libertine which he was, yet wasn't, he followed her unhesitatingly when she turned into the small café-restaurant in the middle of the park. It was empty. The staff stood around grumbling at the weather outside as he followed the girl in. He took a table where he would face her but not too near. Because it was empty, somehow it was impossible to go too close.

He tried not to stare as she removed the gold and green silk and shook out her hair. It was neither black nor yellow, neither very dark nor very fair, neither short nor long. But although the sky was dull and overcast there seemed to be light in her hair.

He watched her order tea and was not surprised that she was beautiful. Her face had a broad dramatic quality. Her eyes were blue-grey, not baby-blue, her mouth wide, full and generous. Her beauty was rare because it did not seek approval. It was a beauty unconcerned with its impact, not careless or haughty but unspoiled by watching for reactions to itself. She did not undo the belt of the drab coat in which he could see now the soft curve of her bosom as she rested her elbows on the white tablecloth.

He ordered tea too and tried to guess more about her. She had glanced his way once but had not lingered over it. She was two or three years younger than he. Perhaps twenty-six. She didn't have an over-emphatic glamour. An actress perhaps. Possibly, but her quiet smile and low unaffected tones with the waitress either belied this or indicated she was a very good one who didn't need to act offstage.

He noticed with a small flood of relief that there were no rings on her left hand. The fact is, he told himself, that she is very lovely and has been dropped into your lap today by the stars in some unusually favourable conjunction. It only remains for you to exert a bit of irresistible charm and away you go together, he thought.

He looked at her slim hands as she held a cup before her and gazed meditatively through a window. Hands that perhaps would hold his a few days from now. Hands that might eventually offer him tea and biscuits, breakfast and dinner, freshly-ironed shirts, Christmas presents, children.

Their eyes met once but hers showed neither interest nor lack of interest, he thought. What did she think of him? Anything? Hard to know what women liked, found attractive visually. Past girl friends had not been much help. One had admitted she'd first been attracted by the back of his head, for goodness' sake! Another, more daring, had eventually admitted she'd noticed he had nice thighs—and that was before they had been introduced. He'd been fully dressed at the time too!

He wasn't handsome but had long since learned that this didn't matter particularly. What should he do now to show himself to the best advantage. Turn his head and gaze through the window directly behind him—and perhaps stick his knees out into the gangway! No, but this was getting serious.

Time was slipping by and the emptiness of the restaurant stood like a barrier between them. How to approach a beautiful stranger in public without the risk of finishing up before the magistrates was a social question so far left unsolved by Britain's cultural traditions. How about the old music hall saw, 'Excuse me, miss, but I am working on the compilation of a new telephone directory, could you please help me by giving me your name, address and telephone number?' Had she got a light or the time? That was worse. Anyway he didn't smoke and a huge clock ticking was the only sound in the quiet restaurant. If only someone would drop a pile of crockery with a loud crash. People winced, screwed up their eyes and shoulders—and smiled at strangers when things like that happened. God! To think the course of his future life, with her or without her, depended on such an unlikely intervention. Could a waitress be bribed to smash? His imagination sometimes became unduly dramatic, he realized at that moment.

She didn't look the kind who would call a policeman in a panic if a stranger addressed her. One of the ironies of a bachelor's life, it seemed, was that he always saw ten times as many beautiful and desirable girls flitting through his life beyond his grasp in streets, buses and tube trains as in socially accessible places like parties.

Suddenly the worst thing in life that could happen was for her to walk out of there and mingle with London's anonymous millions and never be seen again. His pulse-rate leapt at the horror of the thought.

And good grief! Now she was leaving! He made frantic signals to his waitress. The smallest money he had was a pound note. The change seemed ages coming. The belt of her raincoat was still twisted, he noticed in his desperation, as she went out of the door putting the silk square over her hair. Damn everything, he would race after her.

'Please call the police if you like, slap my face, give me a disgusted look, turn on your heel and walk away . . . but the rain, the greenness, don't you think, rather lovely . . . and you're the most beautiful creature I've ever seen and the thought of not knowing who you were or never seeing you again desolated me, please forgive this terrible cheek but what does one do when one sees a beautiful . . .' he would say.

He would blurt it out. He realized—allowing himself a crafty half-grin—it might have a certain charm, the blurting. But it would be real enough because his heart was hammering in his chest now. And here came the waitress at last!

He dashed out. God, the pathway to the nearest gateway was empty. She must have already reached the street and turned out of the gate. Hell, he'd run. It was all important he didn't lose sight of her.

He raced the few yards to the gateway. And skidded panting to a halt. The pavement in either direction was empty. Traffic swirled along the road. He cursed vehemently to himself.

And blast this rain, it was still pouring down!

A beautiful girl in a dowdy raincoat sat in a taxi moving fast in a flying wedge of traffic going down Baker Street. She was thinking of the man in the café in the park. She had felt strongly drawn to him. Just the two of them alone in the café with the rain beating on the windows. As she sipped her tea she had felt certain they would speak. It was hard to say what it was about him that had attracted her. She'd felt him look at her too. Funny thing but when he turned to talk to the waitress she'd noticed something very attractive, something quite undefinable, about the back of his head.

Funny that, she had suddenly and inexplicably felt drawn to walk in the park in the rain. She smiled to herself as the taxi fled on through that same rain.

* * *

A MAN ALONE

Outside the park gates he stared up at the leaden sky. Then after a moment's hesitation turned up his collar close around his ears. And, head down, stamped off along the wet pavement. He was making for the pub on the corner of the street where he lived. A few of the others would be gathering there by now. He anticipated the creamy froth and the bite of the amber ale he would drink with his friends.

The desolation of the flight of the beautiful girl, whom he never saw again, would soon become a vague feeling of something unsatisfactory, then later vanish completely.

Not far away, Fate, a dark figure under the dripping trees, put up his coat collar too. He had turned his back on both of them abruptly a short time before. Now he too strode firmly away—in the opposite direction—wearing the capricious smile we always suspect he wears. He had a thousand more such incidents to arrange before the night was gone. Some similar, some dissimilar. He liked to change his mind—especially at the last moment.

The Play

CHARACTERS:
>Three highly prominent Orient-men.
>Three highly prominent Occident-men.

Three highly prominent Orient-men: Now the thing is this, you see. You highly prominent Occident-men were once very arrogant colonizers and threw your weight about in the Orient. Times have changed. But you've arrested and put in prison some of our Orient-men. We don't give a damn about them but we wish to demonstrate that times have changed and that you can't do it to us because we have appallingly large numbers of people in our Orient country and you are small and now it is our turn to be arrogant. So we have put a poor, fairly insignificant Occident-man in a six-sided cube on his own and will keep him there until you submit to our will. So there.

Three highly prominent Occident-men: Look, I say, this is a jolly rotten thing to do. Well, I mean to say, it isn't even fair. (With a tone of staunchness creeping into their voices.) But we won't be intimidated, you know. We are not entirely unarrogant yet, you know.

A MAN ALONE

Three highly prominent Orient-men: All right, all right, but we are going to hurt him. Nothing absolutely physical, you understand. We are going to hurt him mentally and psychologically though— pretty hard.

Three highly prominent Occident-men: (Even more staunchly.) Huh. Think we can't take it? We can take it all right. We'll show you. It's not us in the six-sided cube you know. We can take it. You won't find us buckling under quickly. It's not us in there.

Three highly prominent Orient-men: Heh-heh, heh-heh-heh!

Three highly prominent Occident-men: (Craftily, with a gleam of self-righteousness coming into their eyes as if they have suddenly seen the way to utilize the right on their side.) Do you know what we shall do if you do not release our Occident-man from the six-sided cube? *We shall cause questions to be asked in our House about you.* And then the whole world shall know how wicked and unfair you are.

Three highly prominent Orient-men: Heh-heh-heh! Heh-heh! In fact, ho-ho-ho! Ho-ho-ho-ho-ho! Do not make us laugh with such pathetic nonsense. Heh-heh, ho-ho-ho! How splendidly democratic.

Questions in your House. Ho-ho-ho! Heh-heh! Pardon us if we do not quake in our shoes in the face of such democratic power.

Three highly prominent Occident-men: (From the saddles of their high horses.) It is only too patently clear to the whole world that your actions are not in keeping with the basic principles of humanitarian behaviour. You shall stand condemned in the eyes of the decent people of the world.

Three highly prominent Orient-men: (In a singsong chorus reminiscent of the fashion in which naughty children defy their weak parents.) We're hurting him, we're hurting him, we're hurting him and you can't do anything about it. You can't do anything about it. We've been hurting him for a long time and you've not done anything about it.

Three highly prominent Occident-men: (Showing some signs of huffy exasperation but refusing to be drawn.) Pshaw, pshaw! Be warned we shall cause further questions to be put in our House about you!

Three highly prominent Orient-men: (Suddenly becoming serious.) You know you people really are disgusting. Really disgusting. You profess to such beautiful ideals of humanitarian sympathy, such sincere regard for every single individual of your kind. And yet for a very very long time you have let one of your kind suffer in that six-sided cube. You are truly disgusting. Now we state quite clearly that everything within the compass of our rule is subordinate to the revolution. It comes first, the individual after. We are true to our principles. Ruthless they are, but we are true to them. But you do not follow your principles. Frankly, we are greatly surprised. We had expected, knowing your principles, that you would help this unfortunate in the six-sided cube. But you have not. For reasons of arrogance and pride ill-befitting such smallness of stature you have ignored him. You are truly disgusting. You surprise us, but you are disgusting.

(Meanwhile, backstage, in the six-sided cube, Christmas has come and the man puts from his mind the characters and circumstances of the play and dreams . . . of a gollywhite. He dreams a gollywhite for Sigmund.)

Gollywhite
for Sigmund

Trelawny Plangrum spilled a large portion of his Sunday breakfast chunky marmalade down the front of his hand-knitted purple chunky sweater. He deliberately stared out at the Hampstead rooftops that glittered with December hoarfrost and tried to remove the sticky mess without attracting the attention of his wife Mathilda, who had recently manufactured the sweater with her own hands—and a pair of knitting needles.

But then, he thought, how foolish it was for a psycho-analyst to harbour a guilt complex over marmalade on a sweater. His mind made up, he suddenly announced in ringing tones: 'I have just dropped marmalade on my sweater, Mathilda.'

His pale, thin wife, scarcely looking up from her Colour Supplement, replied absently, 'Have you, dear? Never mind, I expect it will wash out.'

From upstairs came a regular thumping sound as though something was being thrown repeatedly at a wall.

Trelawny Plangrum poured his seventh cup of coffee, lit his customary after-breakfast Havana

Romeo No. 3 cigar and regarded his wife with a serious expression.

'I have been giving careful consideration to Sigmund's Christmas presents for this year, Mathilda,' he said in a tone not much different from that he adopted with particularly confused patients at the couch-side.

'And I have decided that as he is approaching the age of four, it is time to plan his toys for him with more care and thought for the part they will play in his psychosomatic development.'

The regular thumping from the room above continued.

'Yes dear?' said Mathilda and waited for her husband to continue.

'It is, you know, the practice of most parents to allow friends and relatives to send toys quite haphazardly to their children but I think the time has come to stop this with Sigmund. This year we shall intercept those presents sent to him from others and, I suggest, allow him only to receive the planned programme of toys I have in mind.'

The noise upstairs was louder now.

'I wonder, dear,' said Mathilda, 'whether perhaps you shouldn't go up to the nursery and give Sigmund the lightest of taps on his bottom. He's throwing his bricks at the wall again I think.'

Trelawny Plangrum looked horrified. 'Mathilda, you should know by now that I have never, and will never, physically chastise my son. The risk of incurring his hostility and promoting a preponderant love for you—the classic Oedipus complex—far outweighs any advantage that might be gained. Besides he can do no harm. The sponge-padded wallpaper we have put in there is very resilient and he cannot hurt himself even should he bang his head against it. And the thermostatically-controlled heating unit should ensure he is comfortable enough.'

'Perhaps he *is* banging his head against the wall and not the bricks,' said Mathilda gently.

The psycho-analyst looked sharply at his wife. He had married her because he felt she was an uncomplicated personality. There were times when he thought perhaps he had erred and the explanation was that she was really simple. He brushed back his long brown hair from a broad forehead with quick nervous movements of his right hand, knocking his spectacles askew in the process.

'These are the toys I thought Sigmund should have, to get back to my theme,' he said, jabbing the lighted end of his cigar into his coffee. It hissed briefly, but he did not notice. He stirred the coffee vigorously with the cigar as he continued speaking then laid the soggy object in the saucer, picked up the cup and held it before him absently.

'First, I thought it was time Sigmund had a doll.'

His wife's eyebrows shot up.

'You mean a girl doll for Sigmund,' she said. 'He is a little boy you know, dear.'

'I am quite well aware of my child's sex,' her husband replied testily. 'But the fact is that the libido, although comparatively speaking dormant in Sigmund as yet, should be, in my view, correctly nurtured and this can't begin too early.'

He hurried on. 'Of course it shall be a simply-dressed doll. I don't intend that he should develop a fixation about the . . . um, trappings of femininity.'

'The libido,' his wife faltered, '. . . I forgot just for the moment how you explained that to me before . . .'

'The libido, Mathilda,' he replied slowly, as though addressing a child, 'is the emotional craving behind all human impulse and its repression may cause pathological conditions. It was the term used particularly by the Great Austrian to denote the sex-urge.'

He had been staring out of the window again as he spoke.

'Oh yes, how silly of me,' said his wife. Her face was slightly pink and she kept her eyes fixed on her Colour Supplement.

The thumping from upstairs continued again after a pause as though for rest.

'Anyway the doll will propitiously introduce Sigmund to some notion of the . . . um . . . essential elements of the human condition and so help to avoid needless and dangerous repression or sublimation later,' said Trelawny Plangrum. 'By the way, Mathilda, this coffee tastes a bit strange this morning.'

He nevertheless gulped down the rest of the

contents of the cup, grimaced and continued. 'Another aid to his developing a positive and correctly adjusted attitude in the realm of eroticism.' He dipped his head and took a quick peek at his wife over the top of his horn-rimmed spectacles. 'In psychoanalysis that term is applied to love in all its manifestations, physical, psychical direct, perverted or sublimated. As I say, another aid will be the Reversed Quoits I shall have made for him.'

'Reversed Quoits?' his wife enquired, haltingly. 'What exactly are they, er, dear?'

'I expect you know that quite a common game for children is to throw rings at some kind of upright stem so as to encircle it. I have given considerable thought to the possible effect of the inherent symbolism in this deceptively simple-looking game and have formed the opinion that it may not be without basic influence in causing some young men in later years to approach the important matters of life with diffidence—and possibly with misguided defence mechanisms already built in. I propose to have made a set of Reversed Quoits with one ring fixed to a stationary base and say half-a-dozen stem-type missiles which can be thrown, in an endeavour to make them pass through the ring. Thus the process is subtly reversed and the unfavourable symbolic inference counteracted.'

Mathilda did not understand but did not like to reveal her shortcoming again. Instead she hesitantly put forward an idea of her own hoping it would not sound too outlandish.

'Wouldn't it perhaps be a good thing now to let Sigmund begin to play with some other young children of his age. There are several among our neighbours.'

'You don't seem to understand at all what I intend doing for Sigmund,' the psycho-analyst said, his voice tight with annoyance. 'Before plunging him into the hurly-burly of contact with other persons I intend to provide him with a sound, emotional base for his conduct such as other children don't enjoy. That has not yet been done. What I'm trying to outline to you is a kind of prophylactic treatment for the mind.

'The Great Austrian, as you must remember, Mathilda, held that the class of functional disorders of the nervous system we call neurosis are due mainly to causes associated with repression of the sexual instincts.'

Still the steady pounding noise came from above.

In the nursery the small, dark, pale-faced son of Trelawny Plangrum gritted his teeth and continued hurling his big wooden bricks with careful aim at a particular spot on the padded wall. The surface gave on each brick's impact then sprang back to true with enough force to return the brick to the circle around the boy on the floor.

'If only I could just make a little mark,' he thought to himself staring viciously round the comfortable but bare and undamageable room. But he fancied the spot on the wall he had been attacking for several days now was beginning to weaken.

GOLLYWHITE FOR SIGMUND

Although his little arms were tired from the morning's bombardment, with a determined glint in his eye he continued hurling his blunt missiles.

Downstairs his father explained the remainder of his planned programme of toys to his mother. 'I thought that a Muffled Drum would be appropriate to stimulate his ego yet prevent him from developing the tendencies of the egomaniac. He will be able to beat it as much as he pleases, you see, but being made, as I shall direct, of some soft leather stuffed hard with flock and having only fleece-headed sticks the tumult created by similar toys—which allows the beater to attract undue attention to himself—will be absent.'

Mathilda nodded dumbly.

To make his points with more authority Trelawny Plangrum rose from the breakfast table to pace back and forth before the fire. As he left his chair the tablecloth caught between his thigh and the table leg and he dragged a cup, saucer and plate to the floor with a crash. While his wife squatted to pick up the pieces he addressed her back. 'I've had what I modestly consider a rather good idea for a toy to encourage correct functioning of the super-ego and the mental tendency we call the censor. As you will remember, my dear,' he said heavily, 'the super-ego is that unconscious morality which directs the censor which itself inhibits unpleasant memories from appearing in our consciousness—unless in a disguised state in dreams.'

Mathilda, who had returned to her chair, nodded

obediently again and warily watched her husband pace up and down, anxious to avoid his coming into any further calamitous contact with his surroundings.

'Yes,' he said, 'a rather good idea. I thought I would get Cyrus, that patient-artist of mine, to put together a book of pencil sketches of unpleasant things—say fierce animals snarling, baring their teeth and so on, ogres and giants, shipwrecks at sea, perhaps a road accident or two, that kind of thing. I know what you're going to say, Mathilda, that it's not a good idea to have him copy pictures like that. Well that's the whole point,' he added triumphantly, his voice rising to a shout. 'No pencil and blank drawing book for our Sigmund. Simply a great big India-rubber! When he has looked at each picture he rubs it out, pouf! and it's gone forever!'

Trelawny Plangrum emphasized this last point by tripping over the edge of the hearth-rug. But waving his arms wildly he managed to regain his balance without further disaster. Feeling that his wife was showing signs of an inner battle to sublimate the urge to clear away the breakfast things he hastened to finish his discourse.

'To complete Sigmund's happy Christmas, Mathilda,' he went on, resuming his pacing, 'I propose three more items.

'A wall pennant with the years "1856-1939" simply embroidered on it.'

His wife screwed up her courage and cut in to

ask what that signified.

Letting his voice convey his disappointment in her, the psycho-analyst explained tartly, 'Surely you have not forgotten the man in whose honour we named our son? Those dates mark the life span of the Great Austrian, whose works I hope will play as important a part, nay, a more important part, in his life than they have in mine.'

'Oh yes, of course, what are the other two things, dear,' his wife asked, glancing at the clock and gathering the crockery together on the table.

'I have ruled out toy soldiers, forts, and the like since they tend to accentuate the unwelcome aggressive tendencies. Instead I will have made similar models, but I think of C.N.D. marchers,' he grinned owlishly, 'complete of course with their colourful uniforms, badges, duffle coats and beards. Perhaps some can be in the limp, prone position of passive resistance. And perhaps a small model of Aldermaston could play the part of the fort.'

Reaching the end of his run at the far side of the hearth he swung round and said: 'Lastly, I have been thinking about that Gollywog of which Sigmund has become inordinately fond since he received it from his aunt last Christmas. I believe he has taken it to bed with him every night?'

'Yes dear, he has. He loves his Golly,' replied his wife.

'Well, my dear, have you considered the implication of this obsession? The doll is . . . um . . . black, you know. And there is the unfortunate matter of its name, "Gollywog". You understand? Golly-WOG! This word has a very unfortunate usage in this country and as the question of race relations is to be of increasing influence in Sigmund's lifetime he should not start out with either obsessive prejudices for or against one side or the other. In order to adjust the possible harm already done I intend to replace this doll with one I shall have especially made. Rather than go over too abruptly to a personification of the opposite extreme I thought perhaps a doll, white in hue, but with the similar characteristic rope-like hair and a similar style of dress—in a word I have coined a "Gollywhite". This will make a start in impressing on Sigmund that there is another side to the question.'

He smiled smugly.

'If I understand you correctly, dear,' said his wife mildly, 'wouldn't it be more correct from your point of view to go the whole hog and call it a "Gollywhite-trash"?'

Trelawny Plangrum thought for an instant he sensed a note of sarcasm in his wife's suggestion but finally decided he was over-estimating her.

'No, I think Gollywhite is sufficient for the present. And about the Father Christmas thing. I think it's gone far enough now. He will be four soon, is advanced for his years and is already reading. I propose telling him the truth this year about where the presents come from. He should not grow up in a world of fantasy. He will be very grateful to me for this later as a well-adjusted adult,' he added, planting his foot squarely under the end of the hearth-rug and clawing wildly at the air as he tripped and lost balance completely. His wife, just moving off with the tray of crockery, tried to sidestep but he brought her down too. The noise of the crash momentarily drowned the regular thump of brick against wall from the nursery above.

Had they stopped to listen they would have discovered that Sigmund, having got his second wind, had raised his striking rate to one the Oxford or Cambridge boatrace crews would have been proud of on the Thames—about thirty-two a minute.

Late on Christmas Eve, Trelawny Plangrum took a large white pillow-case and inserted the programme of toys he had planned with so much forethought for his son. As he tiptoed to Sigmund's bedroom, the pillow-case containing the Simply-Dressed Doll, the Reversed Quoits, the Muffled Drum with Fleece-Headed Sticks, Drawings To Rub Out, Wall Pennant 1856-1939, Aldermaston Marchers and the Gollywhite—bumped against his leg.

On the outside he had pinned a piece of paper with a brief message in large block capitals designed to deliver Sigmund from the dangers of growing up in a world of fantasy. 'Sigmund. There is no Father Christmas. That is a Fairy Tale for very young children. These toys are from Your Own Father. A Happy Christmas.'

A MAN ALONE

Sigmund had thrown a tantrum when told he could not take his Gollywog to bed with him as usual. His kicking and screaming had been quietened only at length by his father telling him that before he woke in the morning he would have something much better to replace it and other presents besides, because it was Christmas. Now as midnight struck the psycho-analyst opened the door of his son's bedroom, crept in, deposited his bounty beside the foot of the bed, paused to look, as he felt a father should on such an occasion, with fondness at the tousled head of his sleeping child and stole out of the room.

As his father's soft footsteps died away Sigmund, who had been feigning sleep, switched on the light and jumped out of bed. For a moment he looked as though he was going to cry as he read the note pinned to the pillow-case. But he seemed to fight down the impulse. With lips pursed tightly and the brick-throwing glint coming back into his eye, he reached grimly inside the sack. A look that would have been incredulity on a grown-up spread over his face as he looked at the Simply Dressed Doll.

But he was surprised how easy it was to break off the legs and one arm! The long yellow hair was stupid! How much more stupid she looked bald, he thought as he tugged it off. He stared with a puzzled frown at the next thing out, the Reversed Quoits. A ring fixed to a stick. Huh! But his face brightened when he found that on hitting the doll

GOLLYWHITE FOR SIGMUND

a sharp blow with it, the doll's head not only came off but the ring broke away from the stem too. A couple of thumps on the Muffled Drum with the Fleece-Headed Sticks produced only an almost noiseless 'Pfft'. Then he found that by using one of the pointed Reversed Quoits missiles he was able to slit a hole in the soft leather and hauled out handfuls of flock, flinging them up around him until he was enveloped in a snow-storm of floating fibres. He broke only a few heads off the tiny bearded Aldermaston marchers, carefully setting aside the others to do in the morning. At the sight of the Drawings For Rubbing Out the cold glint in Sigmund's eye changed to a wilder gleam. He was quite still as he flicked over page after page of the snarling animals, tragedies at sea and horrific-looking ogres. Then he hid the sketch book with infinite care under a loose floorboard beneath his bed where he could get it easily whenever he wanted. With equal care he broke the big India-rubber into pieces less than a quarter of an inch square and scattered them. Finally his lower lip curled in contempt as he extracted the Gollywhite, whose name was embroidered on its jacket. He looked at its silly ashen face and stupid white ropey hair. One thing though, it was jolly easy to pick the button-eyes out. And with a single wrench of the legs in different directions there was a jolly good ripping sound. He stuffed the debris around him back inside the pillow-case.

The 1856-1939 Wall Pennant remained unnoticed in the bottom. Sigmund crept out of the bedroom and placed the bulky bag of wreckage against the closed door of his father's room where he knew he was sure to trip over it in the early morning as he went to the bathroom without his spectacles.

'Perhaps he might break his leg,' thought Sigmund, his young face contorting into a dwarf-like mask of viciousness. Or better, his spectacles might smash as he fell and a small sliver of glass might penetrate the jugular vein. By morning he might be found lying cold in a large pool of blood.

And collecting his Gollywog from the living-room where it had been placed earlier out of his reach, he climbed back into bed, put out the light and immediately fell fast asleep. It was already Christmas morning.

The Moon and Storms

When the moon was full each month and shone brightly in through the window the man was reluctant to look on it for long. He could not find a rational explanation for this, except that he realized he was anxious to protect his mind from the unknown. The warders never seemed to notice the moon. They shouted and sang and talked together.

In the height of the summer heat when the gaseous air hung thick and ponderous a storm would often ravage the sky. Hailstones would rifle down and splinter in the yard. Panes of glass in the windows would be smashed. Ice-lumps the size of a child's fist would draw shouts of amazement from the warders. Forgetting their calculated reserve they would rush into the yard to pick up the hailstones. And the man alone would wonder silently at their size too.

After dark one summer night a fierce storm threw down thunder, lightning, rain and hail in a furious onslaught. Lightning struck close by in the street outside. A vivid blue flash and the lights in the entire city went out. The black darkness was lit only by blue lightning. Around the man on his own and around the warders in their room was unfamiliar total blackness. And it went on and on, lit only occasionally by the blue lightning. In their fear and apprehension of the total darkness the warders and their prisoner were briefly united, levelled. Wordlessly at one.

The storm prompts the man alone to dream of rain, thunder and lightning in which a crime is committed—by scientific calculation . . . He dreams of crime and calculus.

Crime and Calculus

Rain slanted down lashing the windscreen of the ten-ton truck as it climbed a steep gradient in the Cumbrian Mountains of northern England. Marty Flowers at the wheel and Alfie Baringer beside him peered ahead as the headlights searched up the wet hillside in the blackness. Both men were far from their regular stamping grounds in London's clubland. Those that knew the two men, including the plain-clothes detectives from Scotland Yard who haunted their world, would have known that only the prospect of rich and dishonest rewards could have brought them to such a place on such a night.

'It's the kind of night Marty when yer wouldn't mind much being warm and snug in yer cell in the nick like the professor, right?' muttered Alfie, a ferret-faced little tough.

'You can go and change places with him in the Scrubs if yer like. But dirty night or not, my palms are beginning to itch as we get nearer Professor Septimus Skyring's hideaway,' the driver replied, his eyes fixed ahead on the upward winding road.

'Yeah, yer right of course. There's gold in these

'ere 'ills—but not for much longer,' said Alfie and sniggered.

The lorry droned on climbing steadily up the highest humps in England.

'I still can't get over 'im giving us the tip-off today on where 'e put the loot,' said Alfie. ' 'Specially after we shopped 'im to get a shorter stretch ourselves. I'll only really believe it when I see those lovely gold bars with my own eyes.'

Marty, craggy of face and build but the more intelligent of the two, thought for a moment before replying.

'Well, you know what the queer old bird said when we first got mixed up with him. How he wanted to apply his scientific mind to get some practical results. Something like that. Seems to me he feels he's going to be stuck away in the nick for a few more years. Rather than have nobody benefit from his ingenious plans, he's tipped us off through the grapevine.'

'Queer bird is right. Funny business from start to finish. Geology professor moving a mountain to rob a train, then stashing the stuff in a rock cavern in the wilds. Not my cuppa tea at all really,' Alfie mused. 'Give me the straight van raid in the Smoke with a stocking over yer face and no messin'. Scientists should stick to their business of blowin' the world up and leave crime to those who know what they're up to,' he said with a cackle of laughter at his own wit.

* * *

Professor Septimus Skyring, professor of geology, had sought out his partners in crime more than three years before in Soho's dimly-lit clubs. He had cut an incongruous figure, tall, stooping, with a bush of grey hair, steel-rimmed spectacles, and shapeless tweeds that hung on his spare frame. Only the intensity of expression in his eyes of palest blue indicated he was a man obsessed. And he soon admitted as much to Marty Flowers and Alfie Baringer.

After watching them intently for more than an hour as they drank and chatted with their cronies, he seemed to make up his mind that these two hard-looking strangers were what he sought. A little nonplussed, they agreed when he invited them to hear a proposition in a quiet pub nearby.

'I believe, gentlemen, in the absolute supremacy of scientific principles applied by trained scientific minds,' he told them in an evenly modulated tone that never changed. 'I am a geologist and have studied the Cumbrian Mountains in north-west England for more than ten years with a greater thoroughness than any one man has studied a high land formation before. I anticipate certain unexpected happenings in that area before long. You see, gentlemen,' he went on, always referring to them as 'gentlemen' although they were clearly anything but, 'in addition to my belief in the supremacy of the scientific mind I believe also in intuition, which I am confident I am able to bring to bear with what amounts almost to scientific application in itself.'

Marty Flowers and Alfie Baringer sipped their beer, looked at each other as if to say 'What's this geezer on about?' and tried to look as though they understood perfectly.

Professor Skyring continued, his pale blue eyes intent upon them: 'But you might say, gentlemen, that I am a man with an obsession. It is all very well working as I have done for the past five years to perfect a new spectrograph with which to estimate the age of the earth more accurately than ever before. But counting isotope ratios in various minerals by this method is satisfying only up to a point. What I wish to do is to demonstrate my enormous, but normally passive, knowledge in a practical way;'—the two villains noticed his hands clenched till the knuckles showed white—'in such a way that everybody will be able readily to understand, the dominant and irrefutably superior quality of the scientific mind in all fields of human experience. In short of the scientific mind of Septimus Skyring.'

Marty Flowers broke in. 'This is very interesting I'm sure, Professor, but would you mind telling us what you're getting at and where two unscientific blokes like Alfie and me fit into your scientific scheme of things.'

'I'm coming to that now,' said the professor allowing himself a quiet smile at their impatience. 'By painstaking investigation in the hills and by mathematical calculations far beyond your comprehension—and with the employment of intuition which is a sixth sense to me as surely as any of your five are to you—I am certain that a large mass of at least one of the Cumbrian hills is on the verge of a slip. I can anticipate its approximate time and even improve on this and precipitate it at a given moment, I believe, with the help in a crucial spot of a detonation. This particular hill overlooks the main Glasgow-London railway line. This fact will allow me I think to satisfy my obsession. All I need to know of is a profitable opportunity when a train bearing valuable cargo is due and I will use my moving mountain to commit a crime unique in history.'

Alfie let out a gasp that clearly implied 'This guy is bonkers.' But Marty silenced him with a kick under the table and asked the white-haired man opposite him to go on. Skyring told how he had discovered a cavern as big as a barn in a nearby hill, that was unknown to anyone but himself which would serve as an unimpeachable hiding-place after the robbery, both for the stolen property and themselves for many months if necessary. He believed bullion shipments from Scottish banks to the London gold market passed along the line and it would be a job within the capacity of two astute men of the underworld like themselves to find out the time of the next one. Stopping the train by putting an English mountain in the way should sufficiently surprise those on it that the three of them could carry off the work without further aid. Any blowing of the bullion car and consequent strong arm stuff—as little as possible, the professor insisted—he believed they could safely handle between the two of them since in fact they were being supported in the crime by what he described as the powerful force of nature, enhanced by scientific control.

Marty Flowers and Alfie Baringer did their part of the preparations efficiently. On the day a shipment of gold bars was due through they met at the home of the professor—a remote house perched on a hillside near Scafell Pike, which rising to 3,210 feet, is the highest peak in the Cumbrian Mountains and in all England. He had obtained a lorry for transporting the bullion. To outline his plan in more detail he drove with the two London men in their car to the spot where later that night he would move the mountain to stop the train. As they drove the professor of geology talked continually, pointing out features of the rugged scenery about them.

'One thing you haven't shown us, Professor, is where the hideout is,' said Marty.

After a slow smile he replied that they must wait until that night to see this final piece of ingenuity, it would be unwise to open it up in daylight, he said. He had provisioned it to enable them to spend several months there if necessary. He was particularly pleased with the construction of the entrance, he said. He had discovered the cavern behind a rock-face that appeared solid but was in fact hollow. To gain entry the first time he had wriggled through a narrow fissure high in the rock face and descended by a rope to the cavern floor far below. Its walls inside were sheer. Working by night from inside he had fitted rollers, hinges and lubrication equipment and detached a frontal slab so that it could be swung back with the slightest pressure like a garage door to admit the lorry. He described to them exactly how it was worked. 'See, gentlemen, how easy things are made for you when working with a finely developed scientific mind,' he added. On the question of their 'cut' in the robbery the professor was vague but assured them he had little interest in the gold for itself. They would be responsible for its eventual disposal and he would make little demand on them. 'This for me is entirely an exercise of applied science—although in an unconvential sphere,' he said.

At a bend in the road a sheer rock face set back from the verge rose above them. A scraggy tree grew out of it high up at a strange angle. 'This formation is particularly interesting,' Professor Skyring began. But noticing the two men were only half listening, and that Flowers, trying to look and drive at the same time, had almost swerved off the road, he did not this time go on.

At the railway line they left the car and climbed high on the bluff overlooking it.

CRIME AND CALCULUS

'This is how I intend to remove what you're now standing on,' said Skyring, his pale blue eyes aglitter. And he explained his plan.

Later that night they stood in heavy rain on the opposite side of the track and a quarter of a mile from the victim hill whose bulk was to be used for criminal purpose. Thunder rolled in the distance.

Earlier, Marty Flowers and Alfie Baringer had watched their mentor slip a charge, that looked ridiculously small to them, into a fissure high on the hill. They had said it hardly seemed possible it would work. Professor Skyring had pulled out his notebook and flipped over page after page of mathematical calculations, then tapped his forehead and said, 'Plus, of course, the essential infallible element, intuition! Have faith, gentlemen, for as I shall show you faith can really move mountains,' and he had laughed a humourless laugh.

Now the bullion train whistled faintly in the distance. Lightning flickered across the sky as the professor fingered the detonator plunger.

'Gentlemen, the master stroke,' he hissed between his teeth. A vivid crackle of lightning rent the skies and in its glare the two men from London's East End saw Professor Septimus Skyring staring upward with wild eyes, the wind whipping his grey hair into a tangled bush that stood off from his head. A sudden jerk of his spare body thrust the plunger downward. They hardly heard at that distance the sound of the single explosion. In the darkness that followed there was no sound but the hiss of the rain—and no movement. Then it was as if the hill looming over the track shrugged itself. In the glare of another streak of lightning they watched in silent fascination as the whole hillside shuddered then swept downward in a solid, tumbling deluge. The ground shook beneath their feet. The rumble and roar of the moving landslide for a time drowned the thunderclaps crashing through the black heavens above. The track was buried under hundreds of thousands of tons of earth and stone as the bullion goods-train rounded a bend a mile away moving full tilt.

The driver began trying to stop half a mile from the slide but the train was still moving slowly when the engine ploughed into the land barrier and lurched off the track. Half the train remained upright including the bullion car. The badly shaken-up guards had opened up the car themselves to see what had happened and due to the shock offered little resistance to the two London thugs as they waded into them with swinging, sand-loaded stockings. The professor drove the lorry alongside, they quickly unloaded the gold bars and he was bumping off along the trackside towards the nearby lane within fifteen minutes. Marty and Alfie ran to their car drawn up a short distance away and followed the lorry's tail lights as Skyring had instructed.

CRIME AND CALCULUS

But at this point Marty Flowers had introduced an unscientific element into the operation. In his anxiety to close up with the lorry ahead he took a corner in the wet lane too fast and skidded into a shallow ditch. By the time the pair, sweating and swearing, had heaved the car back on to the road, the professor in the lorry was out of sight. Within half an hour of the landslide he was rolling back the entry slab and driving into the dry cavern. He was puzzled that the car was not behind but after erasing the lorry-tracks across the grass from the roadside he went inside and closed the slab. The rock face he had begun to describe to his accomplices earlier that day as they drove by it as 'particularly interesting' resumed its normal appearance from outside.

Marty Flowers and Alfie Baringer decided the best thing to do after the mishap was get away from the scene of the robbery as quickly as possible. But the uninjured firemen of the train had run back to the nearest trackside telephone to give the alarm and the two men with criminal records going back several years were picked up in one of several quickly erected police road blocks.

Identified later by the bullion guards the pair eventually elected to make the best of a bad job and turn Queen's evidence; and so they revealed that the professor was behind the whole scheme. But truthfully each said they didn't know where he had taken the gold. Septimus Skyring stayed a week in his cavern—which he had rigged out with camp beds and oil lamps as well as provisions. Air and some light filtered in through the narrow couloir high in the sheer walls through which he had first entered, and a tiny subterranean freshet provided drinkable water at the very rear of the recess. Finally, imagining his two assistants to have returned to London, he walked home across the fells into the arms of the police waiting at his hillside home.

The trial was spectacular and hit the front pages of newspapers around the world. Professor Skyring calmly admitted his intentions and only withheld where the gold, worth £500,000, was hidden. He was gaoled for fifteen years and Marty Flowers and Alfie Baringer, through their disloyalty, got themselves lighter sentences of three years each.

In prison the man who master-minded a crime of science was as incongruous as he had appeared in his brief visit to London's gangland. He spent as much time as he was allowed in the prison library, and there, and even in his cell, he was seen by other prisoners covering page after page of prison exercise books with notes and mathematical calculations. For the first year or two he barely spoke to any of his fellow prisoners. When he did his only interest was to discover what he could about the 'grapevine', the mystery-shrouded lines of communication that exist between prisoners and their cronies beyond the walls. Few people outside the old lags and others who form its links know exactly how it operates. Through it Septimus Skyring heard that his former partners Marty Flowers and Alfie Baringer had been released after some two and a half years. And through it in the reverse direction he sent them a message one day nearly three years after the robbery. Couched in guarded terms that only they would understand he told them it would be worth their while to visit the rock face he had described as 'particularly interesting' where Flowers almost swerved off the road on the afternoon of the day of the robbery. The odd tree would help them identify it. Amazed at this turn of events, the two men immediately got hold of a lorry and headed north from London.

'Yes siree,' said Alfie Baringer, repeating what he regarded as a gem of sick humour, 'scientists should stick to blowin' up the world and leave crime to smart operators like us, eh Marty?'

Marty Flowers did not answer. He was peering out at the rain-lashed road searching ahead for the rock face with the scraggy tree sticking out of it.

'It's——difficult in the dark,' he said, 'but I think we're getting near.'

Then as they rounded a steeply banked bend the lorry's headlights, thrown upward by the steep gradient, picked out the weird tree on the steep rocky scarp.

'This is it, Alfie my boy,' said Marty and swung the lorry on to the verge.

Skyring had explained that afternoon three years ago how the front slab was opened. Searching the rock face with the aid of torches they located the vital crevice within five minutes and forced the slab open. Skyring had surrounded the moving parts with oil containers and it swung open without too much effort.

'Blimey, open sesame,' said Alfie staring incredulously.

'Wouldn't surprise me if we found Ali Baba and his forty Arabian villains in here.'

But inside at the back of a long recess by the light of their torches they found only the bullion still stacked in the robbery truck. The tinned provisions and beds, blankets and camping stove were all there, too, in good order.

'Let's get this stuff on to our truck quick,' said Marty.

He ran out through the downpour and backed their lorry in, closing the slab behind him in case a vehicle passed. The rain splashed down the hillside in torrents carrying mud and pebbles with it. But the dull yellow metal gleaming in the light of their torches as they humped it on to the lorry made the men oblivious of the weather outside. They completed the transfer of the gold in a few minutes.

CRIME AND CALCULUS

'Well, mate,' said Marty grinning at his friend, 'it seems this crazy game has turned out to be worthwhile after all. Shake on it,' he said and they gripped each other's hands, grinning delightedly.

''Ave a fag to celebrate,' said Alfie and offered his packet. Marty took one and leaned forward as Alfie flicked his lighter.

'Keep your hand steady,' said Marty bending his head over the flame, 'I can't get lit.'

'My hand's steady enough, it's the flamin' ground shakin',' said Alfie his voice rising in a shout of alarm that echoed against the rock walls. They stood rooted to the spot with terror as the ground trembled and the cavern was filled with a deafening roar. Pebbles and earth fell in a fine shower on them through the high roof fissure. There was no mistaking the terrifying sounds of a landslide ten times more tumultuous than that at the railway line, since this time they were inside it. Deathly pale and trembling with fear they waited for the cavern's rock walls to collapse around them.

But after minutes that seemed like days the angry rumble of moving earth died away. Then without much hope they tried to move the front slab. It could not be shifted. Outside thousands of tons of earth and stone that had slipped from the shoulder of the pike above their heads engulfed the road for a hundred yards, but the rocky base of the hill remained intact. They sank down weakly on the blanket-covered camp beds realizing that they were entombed. Miraculously it seemed the fissure high in the cavern roof still admitted air. Alfie stared at the tins of provisions. 'We're not dead, but as good as buried alive and nobody knows,' he whispered hoarsely. They sat in silence. Then full realization dawned on Marty. 'Nobody . . . except perhaps one person . . .' he said, staring hollow-eyed at his companion.

In his cell 250 miles away in Wormwood Scrubs Professor Septimus Skyring, professor of geology, sat on his cot, under a naked light bulb, notebook on knees, quietly checking over and over again several pages of calculations and deductions. His pale blue eyes narrowed through their steel-rimmed spectacles and his lips moved slowly. 'Time of the slip—a virtual certainty,' he said to himself half aloud making a little tick on the page. 'Timing of the outgoing message, correlation with likely time required to drive north, search time factor, all right I think,' he breathed. 'Possible delay in slab opening, off-loading, on-loading ingots.' He ticked again and after several more minutes of this, closed the book slowly and rested his eyes. Perhaps he should devise a mathematical symbol, he thought, to represent the intuition quantum which made it unnecessary for him to wait to hear through the grapevine of the strange absence from society of the treacherous Messrs. Flowers and Baringer.

But perhaps a suitable interval should elapse to

heighten the impact on them and others before he revealed their plight to an astonished world.

The Trial

'No,' said the man at the window flinging the book down on the table and getting up. 'You can't go out, you are arrested.' 'So it seems,' said K. 'But what for?' he added. 'We are not authorized to tell you that. Go to your room and wait there . . .'

From *The Trial* by Franz Kafka.*

'From this moment onwards you must remain in your residence and not depart from it . . . That is all we have to say to you.'

From *Hostage in Peking*.**

K. felt he must sit down, but now he saw that there was no seat in the whole room except the chair beside the window . . .

From *The Trial* by Franz Kafka.

The tiny room which I came quickly to think of as my 'cell' was hardly a room at all. It was a space between an outer door leading into the courtyard and the washroom. In it was a bunk on which my

* Published by Martin Secker & Warburg Ltd., 1925.
** Published by Michael Joseph Ltd., 1970.

driver took his siesta and piled around in the room were spares for the car and various pieces of junk.
From *Hostage in Peking*.

They both examined his nightshirt and said that he would have to wear a less fancy shirt now, but that they would take charge of this one and the rest of his underwear and, if his case turned out well, restore them to him later . . .
From *The Trial* by Franz Kafka.

Sometimes the guards would enter my 12-foot room and poke around among my belongings but miraculously they never happened upon my diary.
From *Hostage in Peking*.

'See Willem, he admits that he doesn't know the Law and yet he claims he's innocent.' 'You're quite right but you'll never make a man like that see reason,' replied the other. K. gave no further answer: 'Must I,' he thought 'let myself be confused still worse by the gabble of those wretched hirelings?'
From *The Trial* by Franz Kafka.

'You should confess to being arrogant and impolite to this guard. It would be better if you confess now.' I tried to say as little as possible in reply to the ridiculous accusations of the teenager.
From *Hostage in Peking*.

CRIME AND CALCULUS

K. felt he must put an end to this farce. 'Take me to your superior officer,' he said. 'When he orders me, not before,' retorted the warder called Willem. 'And now I advise you,' he went on, 'to go to your room, stay quietly there, and wait for what may be decided about you ...'
From *The Trial* by Franz Kafka.

I had remembered asking the interpreter how long I was to remain in 'the area designated by the masses' and he had simply repeated the fourth part of the order: 'You must await further notice from the government.'
From *Hostage in Peking*.

Alone in his humourless void, awaiting further notice, the man longed to laugh. He longed to laugh himself—and longed to make others laugh too. And so he dreamed of it. With eyes wide open he dreamed of ... Newton's lore of graffiti.

Newton's Lore
of Graffiti

Mrs. Newton looked across the dinner table at her husband and shuddered slightly.

'Well as the engineer said when the oil drilling rig fell on him, "What a crashing bore!"'

Fred Newton beamed as he said this and followed it up with a short barking laugh. But the frosty faces of the other dinner guests gazed back at him. Unamused. Uncomprehending. A mild inconsequential complaint of some ill-fortune from one of the staid diners had drawn this rejoinder from her husband. Mrs. Newton saw the danger signal. Such an important dinner. He'd been so good until the cheese. Said almost nothing. Passed salt politely to grey-haired old ladies. Now he was making those dreadful puns of his. She knew the pattern of his dinner party humour too well. Puns: what he thought of as his *bons mots*: finally bawdiness. Mrs. Newton shuddered again. Tried to catch his eye, kick his foot under the table, shrank in her seat, waited.

'Speaking of Catholics,' he was saying now. Nobody was, but that didn't deter Fred Newton.

'Speaking of Catholics, the first time I went into a Catholic Church, a priest or somebody came along swinging the little gold incense burner on chains. I stopped him, sniffed, grimaced, nudged him in the ribs and said, "What's that thurible smell?"'

Fred Newton roared. Frosty faces again stared, silent and uncomprehending. Mrs. Newton, in her misery, wondered how many offended Catholics there were among the diners.

The Old Man, she noticed, was watching her husband intently. The Old Man. The Dreaded One. Remote and Caesar-like head of the huge business-combine making paper cups, serviettes, doyleys, wet-strength handkerchief tissues and other paper disposables. The Dreaded One. Sole shareholder of the gigantic family business. A sort of use-once-and-throw-away Alfred Krupp. Giver of abysmally boring dinner parties twice a year. Once every six months. Start 8 p.m. finish 11.30 p.m. Never a minute earlier, never a minute later. Legends of boredom throughout the commercial world. The severity of his presence deadened the spirits of his subordinates. For the dinner parties were only ever attended by his immediate subordinates and their wives. The hoary hierarchy. Invitation to one of these twice-yearly, 8 p.m. to 11.30 p.m. orgies of ennui was a mark of imperial approval from on high. It was Fred Newton's first such accolade.

Some brave soul tentatively broached the importance of harmony of temperament in marriage as a topic of conversation while the fruit was passed round. Fred Newton leaped without looking. 'Very important, if you ask me,' he said loudly. 'Take my wife and me—that's a fair enough offer.' He roared again and looked across at Mrs. Newton who had sunk in her chair. She was mentally deflating, subsiding beneath the table.

'Now my wife is very perky during the day,' he announced to the table at large. 'Dashes around with dusters and saucepans. Very active. But at night she flags, droops. Witness slight indication of that now.'

She coloured and tried to sit up straighter.

'Now me I'm somewhat lethargic by day, but really come alive at night. You see? Our trouble is we just don't speak the same LANGUISH!' He barked with laughter. Looked round at the silent faces. Spelled the word slowly. Barked again. Dug his elbow into a dignified, straight-backed beldame at his elbow. And roared once more. He seemed not to notice the silence that came back from his fellow guests.

From beneath heavy beetle brows the Dreaded One, with a Napoleonic gesture, signalled the withdrawal. And they withdrew, as only English dinner guests in England can withdraw, to take up new positions behind coffee and liqueurs.

'Of course,' Fred Newton continued blithely, 'I don't want any of you to think that this creates a gulf between my wife and myself. I'm all for marriage. As the galley slave of twenty-five years said, glancing down at his wrists chained to the oar, "I didn't like this job much at first but now I've become quite attached to it!"'

His loud, long hee-haws of laughter rattled the coffee cups. One or two of the others shifted uncomfortably, looked towards the Dreaded One. Two coughed. One man grinned sheepishly then wondered whether he should have.

Fred Newton was not abashed. As a matter of fact Mrs. Newton had aimed a bash at him with her handbag under cover of the withdrawal but had narrowly missed. Fred Newton remained, as stated, unabashed.

And Mrs. Newton saw that nice, comfortable, rather expensive London flat—the best they'd ever had—slipping away. The impetuosity of Fred Newton, the super salesman, had brought him crackling up through the use-once-and-throw-away organization like a flash of blue electricity along a wet wire.

A succession of towns. A succession of dreary furnished apartments. Unstability. Now at the dinner that crowned his accession to the throne in charge of sales throughout the disposable empire he was flying in the face of fortune! Mrs. Newton was miserable, perplexed. Not her spouse, however!

'Let me tell you something else about my wife and me, you might find it rather neat,' he was saying. 'I always say that she tries, not quite successfully, to appear to be a gourmet, while I try, perhaps unsuccessfully, not to appear to be a gourmand.'

He dived his hand into a nearby box of chocolate liqueurs, stuffed three into his mouth and looked round expectantly, it seemed, at the frozen volcanoes. But there were no eruptions.

Mrs. Newton, having recognized that the *bon mot* stage had been reached, that the pattern was being followed, tensed herself for the cold plunge into bawdiness.

She didn't have to wait long. Only until her husband knocked his brandy glass to the carpet with a crash.

'Oops. There goes my brandy responding to the law of gravity.' He picked it up and quickly beamed round. 'Which reminds me. I believe there is another natural law that has been at work almost as long as that discovered by my illustrious namesake. I believe I am the first to have formulated it as a principle. Would you like to hear it?'

The guests seemed hypnotized by now and only stared blankly at him.

'Yes, ladies and gentlemen, I am referring to the Law of Graffiti. I define it as: "a mysterious unseen force which impels a chalk or pencil-bearing hand towards a blank wall surface and induces the writing or drawing of vulgarities." I have personally measured the Force of Graffiti in a number of localities and I find it to be at its strongest in gentlemen's lavatories. The word gentlemen being applied in a loose sense, of course.'

Fred Newton rushed on without pause to observe his audience's reactions.

NEWTON'S LORE OF GRAFFITI

'I know what you're all dying to ask. "How did I discover it?" Quite simple. I collect the better examples of the art. I was cutting round a piece of plaster containing an ingeniously disgusting stanza. Rather high up on a lavatory wall it was. It fell and hit me on the head. It was then that I was struck by the existence of a Force of Graffiti.' He kept a straight face.

'I've made a deep study of my subject. Graffiti— an interesting word in itself. Italian of course. First applied to those rude drawings made on the walls of ancient buildings in Pompeii, Rome etc. An interesting modern development in some London pubs is the equipping of the men's lavatories with a blackboard and chalk. Sensible action by landlords. Saves the paintwork. But you see the danger of course? A permanent art becoming an impermanent one!'

He turned to a severe-looking woman on his left who had been staring at him as though she didn't really believe he existed.

'Perhaps you could help me with my research, Madam. Of course, ladies' conveniences being out of bounds to me, I've often wondered about it. What sort of things do you draw on your lavatory walls?'

The shocked and horrified silence was electric. But with a deprecatory wave of his hand he went gaily on.

'Never mind, there's plenty of time. Perhaps you'll think of something. This new impermanence of course is very serious. That's why I've decided to set down my researches in a book, I'm going to call it *Newton's Lore of Graffiti.*' He stopped, spelled the word lore. Had a good laugh. Continued. 'It will be liberally illustrated of course. To give you some idea . . .'

Eleven pairs of startled eyes widened even further as Fred Newton leapt to his feet, plucked a charcoal sketching stick from his breast pocket, and stepping quickly to a blank space on the drawing-room wall, slashed a bold black stroke across its pristine whiteness. Just a single, upward-curving line. But the voluptuousness of the stroke and the leer which Fred Newton turned to his thunderstruck audience gave it a lurid suggestiveness. He turned back, raised the chalk to continue the drawing.

Then the storm broke.

'Newton!'

The voice of the Dreaded One thundered out at last.

The face of the discoverer of the Lore of Graffiti was innocent and querulous as it turned to its host. The charcoal stick remained poised in the right hand.

The Dreaded One, remembering his social responsibilities with a visible effort, swallowed the tongue-lashing he was about to give his impertinent employee. Instead, in a strangled voice, his limbs and shoulders shaking perceptibly, he said, 'It is time everybody was thinking about departing I believe.'

Incredible! 9.45 p.m. Unprecedented! Play stopped with nearly two hours left—because of bad light in which one guest was showing himself.

Coats were taken in a stunned dream by all the guests, it seemed, but Fred Newton.

'Suppose it's a race against time now, sir,' he laughed to his host in the hall, 'whether you sack me or whether I can beat you to the draw with my resignation.' And taking the arm of his stupefied wife he went laughing out into the night leaving the Dreaded One, and everybody else, speechless.

Outside, as they walked, Mrs. Newton, close to tears, asked: 'Why? Why ruin everything?'

His step was brisk, confident, elated. He patted her hand.

'Nothing to worry about, dear. Had an offer two days ago from our big rivals. Said they'd heard how good I was. Same job, more or less, more money. The Managing Director's a good fellow. Got a sense of humour. He'd heard I was attending my first Dreaded Dinner tonight. They're notorious you know. Said he'd heard a lot about my gift of the gab and thought this would be its Waterloo. Gave me a challenge, he did. Said if I could talk my way out of the dinner party before ten o'clock without burning the house down or pretending to be ill he'd put another £500 a year on my salary. Said if I could do it I'd be worth it. He's waiting in a pub round the corner to see if we make it. Come on, it's five to. We'll have to run. I shall have to go over the whole thing for him—all the jokes.'

Mrs. Newton looked at her husband and shuddered slightly.

Newton's Lore of Graffiti of course remains unpublished. Accounts of that dinner party, what was said and drawn, spreading by a word-of-mouth pyramid from that Managing Director have of course become much exaggerated, sometimes absurd. You know how businessmen love to embroider their stories. The only authentic account is the one you've just read. Don't believe any of the others.

No Story

When the man was younger he had trained to be a newspaper reporter. The first thing the older men in the newspaper office had told him was that five questions had to be answered in every story he wrote. What, where, when, why, who? Check before you write your story, son, they said, to see that you have the facts. What? Where? When? Why? Who? And when you've written your story check again to see if the questions have been answered. What? Where? When? Why? Who?

Now, as the man sat in the six-sided cube, alone for a very long time, he knew. He knew that none of the questions could be answered.

What was he? Of flesh and blood. So were dogs. Dissected, the body betrayed no sign of the soul, no sign of the 'I'. Where had he come from, where did he go when dead? Nobody knew. To *what* there was no answer.

Where was he? What was the universe in? Nobody knew. To *where* there was no answer.

When was he? Now. But when was now? So no answer to *when* either.

Why was he? The most clearly unanswerable question of all.

Who was he? Take away the name that had been his since birth and he was a nameless package of tingling blood vessels. Dissect his inert body and there would be no sign of his 'I'. Who was he, indeed?

Five questions. No answers. So there was no story. Because, frighteningly, there was no story the man dreamed that there was. He dreamed that . . . a man was later detained.

A Man was Later Detained

Charlie Cuttright was a sub-editor on a popular daily Fleet Street newspaper and consequently lived his life upside down most of the time. This is to say when others were arriving home after a hard day at the office Charlie Cuttright was just leaving to go to his work. And not long after he arrived home in the black of night to crawl into bed, his wife crawled out to begin a new day with the children. Perhaps this was why life seemed a little unreal to Charlie Cuttright.

Now everybody knows that a sub-editor is not a deputy editor or anything so exalted as the name might imply. He is one of a dozen or more men who sit around a big cluttered table in their shirtsleeves in a noisy room hacking at reporters' stories with thick pencils and writing appropriate headlines on them so that they fit neatly into the ephemeral jig-saw puzzle that becomes tomorrow's newspaper. Charlie Cuttright's life's work seemed to him to centre on composing long ideas into short words in the middle of the night. When a Communist delegate walked out of an international medical meeting in Geneva, Charlie Cuttright, as quick as a flash, could write a headline like: 'Cross Red quits Red Cross'. And become the toast of the sub-editor's table for the evening.

In the small headline-writing world of Charlie Cuttright there were no investigations—only probes. There were no tentative offers or attempts —only bids. No mysterious occurrences—only riddles. Decisions were never rescinded, they were quashed. Attempts were not frustrated but foiled, tribunals would not castigate, they would rap or flay. Life was a succession of vicarious dramas and shocks, rifts and rows, surprises and sensations— which he himself never felt.

So in this nightly jumble of bids, probes, riddles, raps, dramas and shocks, to say nothing of the curbs, ties, pleas, bans, storms and hints that were sought, imposed or made, Charlie Cuttright moved, dealing with the words, but never the stuff, of life.

The few friends his way of life allowed, noticed that he was not left unaffected by his work. His neighbour Stanley Grille who worked in the bank sometimes met him as their paths crossed at the bus stop in the evening, one returning home the other setting out.

'Hello Charlie, how are you?'

Charlie Cuttright was half-thinking of the weather-forecast feature that daily occupied a small bottom corner on page five. It was his regular first job each evening to check it over. He suspected that few people ever read it or understood the little map with wavy lines and arrows.

'Remaining fair,' said Charlie a trifle vaguely. But he always seemed a little vague to his friends. Then he added: 'Temperature averaging 98.4 degrees. Visibility good. Slight depression expected to give way to bright periods later. How are you, Stanley?' He added the last words automatically.

'Fine, just fine. But why the depression?'

'Oh just the regular Monday evening feeling I suppose, nothing more.'

'How's the wife, Charlie?'

'The wife? You mean blonde-haired, blue-eyed, slender, pleasure-loving, mother-of-four Audrey Cuttright, 34?'

'Yes.'

'According to sources close to the Cuttright household, Mrs. Cuttright is in quite normal health. There is nothing that should excite comment of an unusual nature.'

Charlie Cuttright stared somewhere into the middle distance as he spoke. He didn't smile. Stanley Grille never quite knew what to make of his friend.

'And the children, they all right, Charlie?'

'You mean Patrick 8, Eileen 6, Linda 4 and nine-month-old baby John?'

'Yes,' said Stanley who was used to this by now.

'When photographed outside their home earlier today the four rosy-cheeked children were in typical childish high spirits.'

'Oh, you still doing a bit of photography then?'

'Yes, Charlie Cuttright took the pictures.'

'You know Charlie, I sometimes envy you dashing off each evening to handle all the exciting events of the day. Columns of figures are pretty dull beside that. It must be exciting work.'

The bus came then and the sub-editor's reply was inaudible as he got on to be carried away to his weather chart.

He alighted from the bus near Fleet Street. Nobody gave a second glance to the spare, slightly stooped figure going quietly through the darkening streets. His skin was tanned to a milky matt white by the neon tubes that hummed softly overhead each night in the unhealthy fog of stale air and cigarette smoke. The muscles of his arm and shoulders had not become hard and knotted by the years of wielding the sub-editorial pencil. They lay flat, limp and elusive beneath the tight skin of the thin body. A raincoat, slightly frayed at the cuffs, topped a rather grubby sports jacket, slightly frayed at the cuffs. The shirt collar was frayed too and the knot of the rarely-changed tie was beginning to look greasy from contact with finger and thumb. His lank, black hair lay flat along his pale forehead. Like most of the esoteric few who work while others sleep, Charlie Cuttright had come to feel there was no point in dressing smartly. If any employer notices a night-shift man dressing sharp and nattily month after month he should promote him immediately, he is a rare animal!

Charlie Cuttright scarcely saw the streets of London through which he walked, head down, glancing neither right nor left. The shocks, dramas, riddles and probes that occurred daily in these streets, it seemed, from the pieces of paper that leaped unendingly on to his desk from teleprinter machines and typewriters, never happened when he was around in them—so he pressed on unseeing to the office.

It was an average night. He ran an expert pencil over a story of appalling disaster in a far-off land, checked the spelling of the name of the President who had visited the devastated areas, quickly appended the headline '500 Die in Quake Terror', dismissed it to the printers and paused to consume a tomato sandwich and another cup of tea. Sub-editors are cynical men, whose appetites are unaffected by disaster, of which their world of paper is full. The neon tubes hummed, the teleprinter machines clattered, telephones rang, men shouted for cups of tea.

On a story of a girl who, for a dare, dashed on to the runways at London Airport wearing only a flesh-coloured bikini, thus appearing naked and disrupting traffic, he wrote the headlines: 'Airstrip Tease—A Sham Take off'. (He'd told Stanley there would be bright periods later.)

As well as writing headlines he fitted into the larger stories at regular intervals those little cross-headings of two or three words which nobody ever reads. But then they're not meant to register on the consciousness. Sometimes people who don't really read newspapers carefully—most people in fact—catch sight of them and read them half aloud in slightly incredulous voices. Often they are quotes from the paragraph that follows. 'Not all honest' or 'Called policeman dewdrop' or perhaps 'Formula not agreed', 'Clear run', 'Missed lines'. People who really read newspapers carefully— almost nobody—know that they are inserted to make a pleasing typographical pattern. To break up longer stories that would otherwise be a sea of uniform print from which the eye would subconsciously shy away, leaving the story unread.

A form of window-dressing—but they have to be written and Charlie Cuttright was one of the men who wrote them, searching each long paragraph for a little twist of words with which to crown it, knowing full well it was really meaningless. Each crosshead is written on a separate piece of paper marked with instructions to the printer to set it in heavier type. One of the many unappreciated acts of life. This habit of years ingrained in the mind also manifested itself in Charlie Cuttright's conversation, often momentarily puzzling his friends. Sometimes in the middle of a conversation he would say suddenly to Stanley something like, 'No joke'.

And Stanley would say 'Eh? What?'

But Charlie would just go on: 'According to local newspaper reports today there is a strong likelihood of the rates for this area increasing by another 6d in the pound next month. This will be the third successive year an increase has been forced on ratepayers. Reactions from residents can be expected to be caustic. Charles Cuttright of 84 Acacia Avenue will be one of the first to record a protest. "It's no joke" he feels.'

'Oh yes, right you are,' Stanley might say, light dawning at last. But since he was one of the millions who never read crossheads in newspapers he never was aware why they crept into his friend's conversation.

So that night Charlie Cuttright wrote headlines and crossheads—but none better than the striptease one which was acclaimed around the room—and when the panic and rush was over, when the last edition had come sweetly off the thundering machines, its damp ink smudging on the fingers, he went home through what was left of the night and, as usual, slept long into the daylight hours. He didn't dream. He wasn't given to it. Reality was far too unreal for that.

When he awoke Charlie Cuttright had no inkling that for brief moments that day one of the stories-on-paper would come to life before his eyes and under his nose. So he was quite unprepared when, as he walked from the bus towards the office that evening, there appeared some distance along the street before him a group of men with nylon stockings pulled over their faces and coshes in their hands. Because he was unprepared his reactions were unconsidered, reflex.

'Masked Raiders Seen in City Street,' he breathed to himself. He didn't say 'Good grief, what are they up to?' or 'Heavens above, I'd better call the police and get out of here.' He just muttered to himself 'Masked Raiders Seen in City Street' and carried on walking in the direction of the office—and the masked men. Wearing that vague expression his friends knew so well.

He could see now that three masked men had climbed from a car outside a jeweller's shop. And the owner who had been inside was being dragged out and hit about the head and shoulders by one of the men.

'Thugs Batter Jeweller in Gems Snatch Bid' he muttered grimly through his teeth as he drew nearer.

The crash and tinkle of breaking glass followed as one man smashed open the shop front. 'Thieves Grab Big Diamond Haul in Daring City Raid' he murmured, quickening his pace as he came up to the scene. The men, their faces appearing grotesquely misshapen under their masks, were working fast scooping things from the window. They ignored the startled people in the street. The jeweller was slumped on the pavement.

Charlie Cuttright by this time was up to them. Unlike the remaining smattering of passers-by he did not hesitate. 'Lone Bystander Battles Gems Raiders,' he hissed suddenly, lunging forward.

One bandit half-turned in surprise at the sight and sound of this pale, thin man coming towards him. 'You what?' he said, startled.

Charlie Cuttright paused and repeated himself, almost plaintively: 'Lone Bystander Battles Gems Raiders.'

'What you?' the bandit asked, surveying Charlie Cuttright's undeniable frailty and grinning.

Charlie Cuttright hesitated. But the headline was already there. There had to be a story. No story, no headline. 'A slightly-built by-stander took on three surprised, cosh-wielding gems raiders as they carried out a daring smash and grab in a city street last night,' he said, his voice rising to a defiant shout.

And he was as good as his word, hurling himself bodily against the doubting bandit.

'He grappled with one man as the masked thieves scooped gems from the broken shop window. The shop owner who was set upon by the raiders lay unconscious nearby,' panted Charlie Cuttright as he staggered and struggled.

'Crosshead "Curb K.O."' he intoned through tight lips.

'What was that?' hissed his opponent, trying to get in a blow at Charlie's head with the cosh.

But the sub-editor was not going into the esoteric question of crossheads just then.

They swayed and struggled, but Charlie was hardly strong enough to do any telling damage. Then suddenly the bandit tripped and fell, struck his head on the curb and knocked himself cold.

'One of the bandits was downed and knocked

unconscious when his head struck a curb-stone,' grunted Charlie unnecessarily, breathing heavily.

The masked man was to spend long hours in his cell wondering how that strange, pale, thin man had known beforehand he was going to clobber himself on the curb.

Charlie would have wondered too if he had thought about it. But he didn't. He was still in a reflex action. The other two crooks had seen it was time to take a hand. They rushed at Charlie together, coshes swinging. And collided with each other. And staggered back stunned.

'In the mêlée that followed the plucky bystander leapt to the bandits' car parked at the roadside with its engine running and doors open,' roared Charlie Cuttright, doing same. 'He astutely plucked the keys from the ignition and dropped them down a kerb-side drain,' he panted, likening deed to word.

When he turned and looked up the two conscious masked men had decided to cut their losses and run for it leaving their less fortunate colleague prostrate. Now other people were running, whistles were blowing, men were shouting.

'New headline,' yelled Charlie triumphantly. 'Unknown Passer-by Foils Gems-Grab Gang.' And he ran too—in the other direction. By the time he got to the office his breathing had returned to normal, the thumping of his heart and the shaking of his limbs had ceased and he was calm again. The cluttered surroundings of the sub-editors' room under the glare of the neon tubes were comfortingly familiar. Perhaps the other thing had been a figment of his imagination. He got on with the weather chart and was soon trimming and amending, headlining and crossheading, measuring and planning, contributing to the night's jig-saw with his usual skill.

He was half-way through a piece one of the reporters had brought in, swiftly dotting i's and crossing t's with a robot-like precision, when he suddenly broke out in an ice-cold sweat. The reporter had begun by saying an anonymous hero had risked his life in a London street that night in preventing a robbery. Charlie Cuttright's professional eye had slipped quickly over the words to about half-way before recognition of the circumstances dawned on the inner man. Then with shaking hands he went back and read how the anonymous hero, according to eye-witnesses, had floored one robber before slipping into the car to grab the ignition keys. The eye-witness had watched horrified as one of the other thugs drew a revolver and pointed it at the back of the man leaning into the car. At the last moment, his partner-in-crime seeing the keys were lost, knocked the gun aside and tugging at his sleeve persuaded him to run instead. One odd thing the eye-witness noted was that the hero shouted incoherently throughout the incident.

Charlie Cuttright was trembling now. 'A man was later detained,' the story said finally. That would be the unfortunate who'd hit his head on the curb, thought Charlie. The reporter knew his stuff. Newspapers couldn't say that one of the thugs was later detained since this would prejudice the eventual trial. No matter how obvious the link was, the formula had to be stuck to in order to conform with the law.

A colleague at Charlie Cuttright's elbow was regarding him strangely.

'You all right, Charlie?' he asked finally.

'Well, er, I feel a bit dicky. Would you mind doing this piece for me? I'll be all right in a moment.'

The colleague took the story and looked through it.

'You must be going soft, Charlie,' he said, making a joke of it. 'There isn't even a single death in this one—only a near miss.'

Charlie tried a smile that came out lopsided.

'Could almost be you though eh, Charlie, this pale, thin hero with the dark hair?' He laughed again at the very idea of it.

'Don't be ridiculous,' said Charlie.

But suddenly, although by delayed action, life had become real for Charlie Cuttright. And for a time the paper dramas that passed through his hands took on a faint aspect of flesh and blood.

But it didn't last long. Nothing else ever happened to him and before long he could again write a headline like 'Seventy Missing in Maze Blaze' and bite directly into a tomato sandwich without loss of appetite.

Epilogue

The seven stories which form the basis of this book are selected from thirteen stories written in confinement in the heat of the Peking summer of 1968. Then I was held under close guard in a bare-floored room twelve feet square furnished only with a bed, a table and a chair. I had been a prisoner for nearly a year then, isolated completely from the outside world, and was to be a prisoner for a further year after I wrote the last story.

The object of writing the stories was to occupy my mind and eyes and hands, but mainly my mind. The inexplicable dreariness of day-to-day confinement doesn't give a solitary prisoner any elated feeling that he is enjoying a sustained visionary experience. But there are moments when there is a strong feeling that the completeness of isolation, the total separation from all normal, practical social activity and movement have brought him closer to glimpsing what are often lightly referred to as eternal truths.

But confinement in a solitary state requires a return to a normal crowded human environment

EPILOGUE

to put it in perspective. Until then the experience is unfinished, incomplete. Now, back in an unconfined world, living in the peace and tranquillity of Jersey in the Channel Isles, in a charming eighteenth-century granite farmhouse, it seems much clearer that in many ways one was pushed out on to a metaphysical limb. That one's contact with mundane reality was more tenuous. The limb might well have cracked and sent one tumbling down into a new, undreamed of and infinite dimension of existence.

I find myself lapsing into the use of the stylistic 'one' as in the last paragraph frequently in reviewing the experience. And I have done it deliberately there, since looking back from this distance there is a strong feeling of it all having happened to someone else. There is this strong desire to draw off and look down and back at the individual to whom it happened. Maybe this has something to do with being a journalist, normally preoccupied with observing and commenting and reporting on what is seen, heard and surmised. Or maybe it is because the experience is past and remote and all that remains is the vast difference it has wrought on my feeling for life, my attitude to life and in fact what I do in life. For one thing is certain. The confinement alone was only half of it. The other half is the life that follows it, and changed reactions to things, clearer awareness of what's important and what's not—all positive and beneficial things out of a negative and sometimes harrowing experience.

But to return to the stories. They were written in three exercise books in very small handwriting so that the limited space was utilized to the full. I was allowed an exercise book after eight months to write my first letter home. By pretending I had exhausted the book when the time came to write the next letter—different guards were then present —I got another exercise book. By the same method I got yet another book a month later. This last one was a hard-covered, thicker exercise book in which my Chinese translator in normal times had kept a record of money spent on postage stamps in my office. So I built up a store of paper unknown to my guards.

The stories were written without the guards knowing, starting in May, 1968. Very frequently I had to hide the exercise book and pen as a guard approached the room across the bare floorboards of the corridor outside. I kept the propaganda material I was allowed, ready at all times to cover up what I was doing. Eventually this became a nerve-wracking business and was one of the reasons why in about September I stopped writing and hid the books away. Another reason was that after writing thirteen stories I felt no further ideas were left in me. Because I was so cut off I had no more stimulus to write further—until I had 'lived' some more to give me more fuel to write with. Also I began hoping, wrongly as it turned out, that I was going to be released and I put these means of survival behind me. When I began to renew my efforts

EPILOGUE

to endure the isolation after coming out of the despair of disappointment at not being released, I hit on other methods and never returned to writing stories.

I kept them hidden until my release and I was able to bring them out of China undetected after over two years of confinement. Now beside me on my desk in the comfort and security of my own home the dog-eared pages, the spindly, cramped writing with a fine-nibbed ink pen look incongruous. The cheap exercise books that once bore a picture on their paper covers of a Chinese studying the works of Mao Tse-tung are a flimsy reminder of another world. The black, hard-covered postage stamp book of my translator, Mr. Wu, is of paper of a stiffer, better quality. In it I achieved a neatness and roundness and consistency of handwriting I had never achieved before in my life and certainly never since. In the quiet long hours and days of isolation, even my handwriting, erratic since birth, took on, by necessity, a disciplined appearance.

I was able to write clearly and neatly because I never started to put pen to paper until the evening when the guards were settled down for the night on camp beds and on the couch in my dining-room. Then only one was on active watch and the chance of them coming into my room through the ever-open door was less. But I spent all day 'writing' the next passage in my mind over and over again, correcting and pruning before setting it down. I wrote an instalment each day, several hundred words at a session. As an entertainment it was rather like a serial story in reverse. I made myself wait until the next day, not before being able to read the next instalment, but before allowing myself to write it.

The stories were not conceived as a book. Only as an occupation, an entertainment for myself, dreams with which to endure time alone. I have put them together here with the thought that it might be interesting to show the reaction solitary confinement found in me. They were defence mechanisms. But they were also experiments in a sense in trying to set down ideas in an entertaining way. Although the enjoyment of writing them was largely mine they were, too, I suppose, an expression of subconscious faith in my eventual release since I always hoped they would be read by others. Apart from a few half-hearted attempts at writing short stories in my late 'teens I had never written anything beyond news stories and articles for publication.

The theme linking the stories was inspired by various vivid moments of thought that occurred during my confinement in Peking. I 'wrote' four of these linking passages in my head while sitting alone there, but set them down for the first time on paper only some months after my release. The 'Man alone' passage was the first of these and when I came to write it down I had no difficulty in calling the words from my memory, so strong still was that

EPILOGUE

feeling of sitting in a loaded dice. 'What is the universe in' was another passage I wrote over and over in my mind while a prisoner—as was 'No story'. The other piece written from memory was 'The Play' which expressed the bitter view of my circumstances I had alone in the small room. To this it was all reducible, I felt, a childish and nonlaudable level. I still feel it is worth reproducing as a point of view. The other linking passages are shreds of thoughts from that long time alone, before release and a new involvement with life brought a bombardment of new impressions and thought chain-reactions.

Perhaps in the stories themselves there was a subconscious expression of the things that confinefent alone made me think. While the days, weeks and months and years dragged slowly by I was also paradoxically conscious of the swiftness of time. Because the days were empty, the sun rising and setting, getting up and going to bed, spring summer autumn winter and spring summer autumn and winter again—sometimes all these things seemed to be flickering across my vision like a speeded-up film. The fleetingness, the brevity of life was borne in on me very strongly and made me reassess my ideas of what was important and what was trivial.

But at the same time there was a sense of continuity, a sense of a life force which would continue despite the shortness of the lives of the individual units of that force. The inevitability of the seasons and the sun and the turning of the earth seemed to assert that human and animal life and plant life too are only expressions of something which is common to all, which is at the basis of everything. This idea is most strongly expressed in 'The Old Man and the Leaves'. The similarity, the relativity, the questions of scale and comparison are there too in 'Himself'.

I had a tree in my yard and watched it every day in every season and in every mood. I watched the leaves and thought of their different life-spans and appearances as being similar to the appearance of people en masse. When rain drenched the yard during my normal exercise period I was still allowed to go out but instead of walking I stood under the curved roof of the gate to the street, watched intently by a guard from only yards away. Forty minutes would pass in this way with just the sound of the rain in the yard and our eyes meeting uncomprehendingly every so often. In this bizarre circumstance I came to watch endlessly the rain driving down into the puddles, the bubbles springing up and eddying around and this led me into the opening of the piece called 'To Cut a Long Story Short'. The short-lived bubbles seemed very strongly to represent people on the world in their spontaneous creation, their pointless, erratic movement on the surface of the puddle in response to the blows of other raindrops, in their interaction with each other. While it rained the puddles were a frenzy of activity, then when it stopped all was calm and still and nothing again.

EPILOGUE

I felt a great need for laughter and humour of which there was none in my life. I wanted to scoff, we all need to scoff, it reassures us, and I wanted to be made to laugh and I wanted to make others laugh too. Perhaps this shows through in several of the stories but not more than in 'Newton's Lore of Graffiti' and 'Gollywhite for Sigmund'.

The gap between reality and the way that reality is represented in public media like television and newspapers—and even history books and legends—is something that has become more forcibly clear to me than ever before, since returning from Peking. But in 'A Man Was Later Detained' an instinctive feeling for this caused me to write what was for me at least the most amusing tale of all. Only since my homecoming have I become fully aware of the very serious foundation the story has beneath the humour.

The verse that makes up the prologue was written in my head just before Christmas 1968. It was inspired by the sight of a gecko—an Asian wall-lizard—near the warm pipes in my washroom. As I turned the creature's name over in my idle mind the name of El Greco sprang forward to rhyme with it. Picasso and lasso followed in the same moment and before I knew it I was launched on a project which occupied me for several days off and on.

Looking back, that strange little doggerel seems to epitomize for me some of the strengths and weaknesses of a man alone. Pathetically without occupation or purpose yet striving with the only resources at his disposal, his thoughts, to imprint some design on the emptiness of time, to amuse himself, to bring something out of nothing. If it isn't putting too high a symbolism on it, it seems to be a microcosmic representation of what art is to man—a filling of the meaningless void with some meaning, albeit contrived. In the same way I moved the chair at which I said prayers on Sundays. Each day of the week I left it at the side of the bath. On Sundays I moved it out into the middle of the bare bathroom and prayed there. In this way I gave a rhythm to the week, seven days then start again. The ritual gave life some form, a shape, a pattern. I was imprinting something on the void.

There are only two features common to all the stories which otherwise appear to be a hotchpotch. One is that they are all set in London, the other is that none of them ends disastrously. The London setting was clearly an escapist expression of my longing to be there. Most of the rest of the thirteen are set in London too. Often I began the germ of the idea for each story by casting around then building on a situation in which I would have liked to have been in London. And so sensitive was I to the possibility of total disaster for myself—not necessarily sudden death but more likely a slow lingering disintegration in isolated confinement—that I could only bring myself to pen agreeable finales to my stories. The suggestion of a grisly

EPILOGUE

ending to 'Gollywhite for Sigmund' was added only after I got home from Peking. And then it stopped short of the violent death I had originally thought of for the anti-hero when I first conceived the outline in Peking. The feeling lingered on!

In deference to my captors and the possibility that they would find the exercise books and go through the stories with a fine toothcomb, I took certain precautions. I dated each day's production so that the manuscripts were broken up every few hundred words with dates. I quickly realized this would give away that I had written them in confinement—possibly against the guards' wishes and rules. So I put the year before's date on them, May, June and July '67, so that if they were found I could claim they were old stories I had written before I was put under house arrest. Where there was a semi-derogatory reference to a Communist in 'A Man Was Later Detained'—a funny headline 'Cross Red quits Red Cross'—I changed this to a nonsense to avoid giving offence to the over-sensitive Communists guarding me. I made it 'Cross Road quits Road Cross'. In 'Himself' I changed the sexual references too. The atmosphere in China today is officially fiercely puritanical. The official media constantly condemn the bourgeois decadence of the West. Somehow in this atmosphere I wasn't able in 'Himself' to use the terms Glamour Department and Reproduction Unit for the part of the man's body I was referring to. Instead I made it the Gambling Department (perhaps even funnier really!) and the 'Unit producing white corpuscles situated in Femur'. I made similar changes in other stories. For a while I was frightened to write 'Himself' at all. For since the whole story was set in the parathyroid glands, I began to worry I would become obsessed with my own parathyroid glands in my throat, would not be able to stop thinking about them, and would imagine all kinds of things going on in there. In the end I decided to chance it—and was delighted to find I so amused myself writing the story that I never thought to be obsessed with my own glands!

Jersey, Summer 1971

Author's Postscript
Summer 2003

Those few lines at the end of my 1971 Epilogue which describe how I overcame my fears about writing the story *Himself*, remind me in this year 2003 just how much my thinking has changed since then. As I have already indicated briefly in my Preface, the chief aim in writing the new material for this republished book is to show how echoes of my experience as a hostage in China - and what I felt and wrote about it at the time - returned some twenty-five years later to help reshape my life and understanding in a profound way.

That will lead to my conclusions about the weighty topic of our human connections to extraterrestrial life in the universe beyond our solar system. Yet before I begin to describe that in detail, I will confess to having another reason for writing this Postscript: and that is to update briefly my own experiences over the past thirty odd years for those many people all over the world who were kind enough to concern themselves at the time with my fate during the two years and two months I spent as a hostage in China.

Although paperback editions of both *Hostage in Peking* and *A Man Alone* were republished in l988 and l990 respectively, following my first return visit to China in twenty years, at that time nothing at all was added to the original texts of either book. From enquiries I have continued to receive in readers' letters it has become clear that there is a legitimate curiosity about what has happened to me since the books were first published in 1970 and 1971 respectively.

In providing this update it gives me a fresh opportunity to say a heartfelt 'thank you' to all those many thousands of people in many countries who cared and showed concern. Many tried to send me letters and cards whilst I was held in Peking - which the Chinese authorities always intercepted and burned by the sackload - while others wrote to their newspapers or their elected representatives in their own countries and became activists on my behalf in other ways. Discovering after my release that all this had been happening on a wide scale without my knowledge was a major factor then in restoring my battered faith in human nature.

The overall purpose of this update then is to give a broader perspective to my Peking experience and all that has followed - and perhaps the best way to do that is by tracing briefly the fortunes of my subsequent writing career from the penning of these initial short stories in China through to the present day. I will confine myself here to professional matters and deal with more personal details in the Postscript to *Hostage in Peking Plus*, which is being simultaneously republished alongside this book.

I have already indicated earlier that profound implications for me were contained in the short passage of philosophical reflection entitled *What is the Universe In?* which introduces the second story of the collection entitled *The Old Man and the Leaves*. However, *Himself*, the first story in this collection and the very first one I wrote in Peking, is also a significant part of this explanation.

After *A Man Alone* was published, *Himself* seemed to take on a life of its own. It was first published worldwide in the prestigious, if racy, Playboy magazine; then because the story's biological foundations were apparently sound, and it was also humorous, *Himself* was published more satisfyingly in a serious medical magazine circulated largely among doctors in the United States. I later adapted the story as a script for a radio play which was broadcast on the BBC in Britain and this led to the London Nightingale School of Nursing adapting the play for the amateur stage -- and for some years I understand its student nurses produced it regularly for mixed purposes of education and amusement in end-of-term performances. To my surprise and delight the radio play was also later broadcast in several countries from Switzerland to Australia.

The idea for *Himself* - which jokily presents the billions of cells in our bodies as minute intelligent individual human beings caught up in boring governmental, industrial and bureaucratic lives - came to me in a flash at the age of seventeen. At the time I was out enjoying a bout of wild, underage teenage drinking on the way with friends to a Saturday night dance.

As we recklessly downed pint after pint of beer, I mimed a comic vision of vastly overwhelmed human chemical process workers throwing up their hands defensively inside our stomachs as repeated cascades of alcohol showered down all around them, much faster than they could open their sluice gates and ducts to channel the deluge to the right digestive zones. After a brief burst of hilarity, the idea submerged itself completely until it resurfaced effectively more than ten years later in the head of a desperate hostage in China.

It is perhaps worth adding briefly here that I had originally decided very optimistically at the age of nineteen to become a writer of fiction. That decision came well before I developed the ambition to be a newspaper reporter. So writing fiction, I feel I should admit, was not something that occurred to me for very the first time when I was a hostage.

Whilst I was serving in the Royal Air Force in Scotland in 1957 after being called up among the last batch of National Servicemen, I had written one or two very unremarkable short stories. I received the rejection slips from magazines that these stories richly deserved and decided as a result that it would be best to learn a bit more about life before trying to write meaningful fiction.

I deduced then that the fastest way to get into print each day was to become a reporter: learn something more about writing and get published daily at the same time! I managed to get some spare time reporting work in the evenings and at weekends on a new and tiny weekly newspaper published in the suburbs of Glasgow, called the *Bearsden and Milngavie Chronicle*. My first and only front-page by-line story with the *Chronicle* under the snappy headline 'Water Water Everywhere!' was a report on an exhibition mounted at a local waterworks! Humble stuff, but I was on my way and I left Glasgow a few months later after cutting my journalistic teeth in this fashion.

During the next ten years or so with the *Eastern Daily Press* and then Reuters, I became totally absorbed by seeking and reporting the news and completely forgot about my ambition to write fiction - until that desperate summer of 1968 when I had been a hostage in Peking for nearly a year. Then I was at my wits' end, casting about frantically for something to combat the threatening void of fear, lengthening isolation and depression in which I was caught fast.

Writing fiction, albeit secretly and stressfully under the ever-watchful eyes of the guards, became for me a great salvation. It also provided a very important discipline and focus for my thoughts and reflections. Also, looking back from this vantage point in 2003, it is clear that writing those stories helped not only preserve my sanity whilst I was being held in solitary confinement, but they also changed the direction of my life very substantially after my release in October 1969.

Back home in freedom as I gradually recovered my equilibrium I found I had changed greatly. I had lost my super-keen appetite to be a newshound, always straining at the leash to be off following the world's latest and hottest news story! I had become more reflective, philosophical, more inclined to look deeper into the obscure, longer-term meanings of life rather than to write always about the simpler facts of developing daily events.

After spending two or three weeks in London in the glare of the world media spotlight following my arrival home from Peking, I flew away to the peace, natural beauty and tranquillity of Jersey in the Channel Islands to begin writing the book of my experience, which I called *Hostage in Peking*. I was desperate to empty myself of all the tension and trauma of those two years as fast as possible and I had fully completed the 350-page book in six weeks of furious writing by the end of February 1970. It was first published in Britain in September that year.

I married my girlfriend Shirley McGuinn in Jersey in April 1970 and we decided to set up home in the beautiful, secluded island principally because it provided the soothing sense of balm we both needed after the traumas of the past two and a half years. There were also some tax advantages to be gained by not returning immediately to live in the United Kingdom itself following five years abroad with Reuters. So we lived in the island until late 1973 when we returned to live in London and I began broadcasting on the BBC World Service from Bush House in The Strand, presenting a daily current affairs programme, *Twenty four Hours*.

During our time in Jersey I had prepared the original edition of this book for publication in 1971, selecting seven from the 13 China short stories that I felt were most worthwhile. To my delight they were published in book form by Michael Joseph Ltd to 'deepen the picture already given in *Hostage in Peking* of how the author survived his ordeal'. I also later selected around 60 of the 300 crossword puzzles I had created as a hostage for a paperback book of puzzles, which was eventually published by Penguin in 1975 as *Crosswords from Peking*. That some of the things I had created to fill the void of many empty days became useful and rewarding after my release helped counteract the great feelings of waste and futility that had often seized me during my innocent captivity.

Before I left Jersey I also quickly wrote a first novel to see if I could make the transition from short stories to longer fiction. It was called initially *Some Put Their Trust in Chariots* - and in later paperback editions *The German Stratagem*. It was a chase-spy thriller with a freelance journalist hero, Jonathan Robson, telling his story in the first person. The novel was set against the background of both my Cold War experiences in East Berlin and the contemporary tax haven setting of Jersey. Again I wrote it in six weeks but it was only moderately successful, carried somewhat perhaps by the media publicity worldwide I had received as a hostage.

Back in London while presenting *Twenty Four Hours* on the BBC World Service two or three times a week I wrote another spy thriller set in eastern Europe called *The Bulgarian Exclusive*, starring the same journalist character. Again I was using the background experience of having covered communist Eastern Europe for Reuters, but this time I switched the narrative to the third person. This second novel was published in 1976 and to my delight it was published in the United States as well as Britain. A third thriller, somewhat more serious and set in China was called *The Chinese Assassin*. I dropped the journalist Robson and invented a new protagonist, Richard Scholefield, a tough minded academic with a background in China studies.

Published in 1978 on both sides of the Atlantic, it was set against the real-life disappearance in 1971 of China's Defence Minister Lin Piao, who was alleged by China's Communist leadership to have tried to assassinate Mao Tse-tung before dying in a plane that crashed in flames in Mongolia as he reportedly tried to flee to the Soviet Union. I researched as best I could what had really happened to Lin Piao via some contacts in intelligence agencies in Washington and other places and wove the results into my novel. My findings, however, were not conclusive by any means.

At about this time while I was reading the proofs for *The Chinese Assassin*, a fellow presenter of *Twenty Four Hours*, David Holden, who was then the chief foreign reporter of the Sunday Times, disappeared in Cairo and was eventually found dead with all labels cut from his clothing to make identifying him difficult. It seems likely he was murdered by intelligence agents of one country or another in the Middle East political cauldron for reasons that have never become clear. I had to take over some of David's spots on the BBC broadcasting schedule whilst he was missing and after his body was eventually found languishing anonymously in a morgue, I suddenly felt disenchanted by the prospect of writing further spy thrillers for the purposes of entertainment when the reality of such things so close to home could be so brutal and shocking.

This feeling led me to turn to writing more serious historical fiction and I ceased radio broadcasting altogether to become a full time novelist. I spent the next four years between 1978 and 1982 writing *Saigon*, an 800-page historical epic dealing with events in Vietnam between 1925 and 1975. *Saigon* became a best- seller in several countries, most memorably entering the Australian best-seller list at No 1 whilst I was there on a promotion tour.

The media reviews internationally were a writer's dream come true and I was inspired to go on to write a second modern historical novel *Peking*, set against the background of China's turbulent history between 1921 and 1978. The story linked the Long March and the Cultural Revolution and writing it occupied me for another four years between 1984 and 1988. This novel too was very generously received on both sides of the Atlantic and in Australia, South Africa and Latin America.

In 1983 in between writing *Saigon* and *Peking*, I rapidly wrote a non-fiction book about Harold Holt, the Australian prime minister who disappeared into the sea off Portsea, Victoria in December 1967. I came by information demonstrating to my satisfaction that Harold Holt had effectively spied for Communist China for many years although he was seemingly motivated by a strong personal conviction that helping the Peoples Republic of China was in the long-term interest of both Australia and China.

Entitled *The Prime Minister was a Spy*, the book was controversially published in Britain and Australia in November 1983 against a great media barrage of criticism and disbelief without any substantive evidence being produced to undermine the book's thesis and its strong circumstantial evidence. The criticism of the book was almost certainly orchestrated by Australia's government and intelligence services. I still stand by the material presented in the book. Soon there will be an opportunity to present more evidence I have discovered since the book's publication which support and amplify its basic revelations and conclusions.

The year 1988 was something of an *annus mirabilis* - a miraculous year - for me. Not only was my novel *Peking* published to acclaim in the autumn, but I also returned to China for the first time since my incarceration as a hostage - an experience which I found fascinating. I also travelled to Vietnam for the first time ever and visited all the major scenes of my novel that I had only able to envisage in my imagination until then.

In the Chinese capital first in January on a research trip and again in June for filming, I was given a warm welcome by the Chinese government after receiving an apology from the Chinese Embassy in London for what had happened to me between 1967 and 1969. I went to make two one-hour television documentary films back-to-back for the BBC entitled *Return to Peking* and *Return to Saigon*. In the China film I compared the country I had known in the 1960s with the vast changes I found there in the late 1980s and revisited with film cameras the house where I had been held hostage.

In other highlights I had a warm reunion with Sao Kao, my former Chinese cook and discussed the past with some cordiality with those Chinese officials who had been involved in my imprisonment. The feeling of reconciliation that these experiences produced will live long in my memory. To return to a greatly changed China and move about the country relatively freely as an ordinary and unmarked man was a very gratifying experience; to be honoured at an official Foreign Ministry banquet and receive official gifts from the New China News Agency and Peking Television and Radio staff came as a very pleasant additional surprise.

In Vietnam we became the first foreign film crew to fly into the old colonial battlefield of Dien Bien Phu since the ill-fated French bastion fell there in 1954. The fondness I had felt for Vietnam while researching and writing *Saigon* in France and the United States was enhanced enormously by at last seeing that very beautiful country and its people for myself at first hand.

The Communist authorities had turned down all my requests for visas whilst I had been preparing the novel so it was the greatest pleasure to be able to travel the length and breadth of Vietnam at long last during the research and filming trips. I learned from Vietnam's Minister of Broadcasting that my novel had been translated into Vietnamese by the government for use in teaching officer cadets history at the People's Defence University in Hanoi. I was truly touched since I had already learned with great surprise that the novel was being used as a teaching aid on history courses organised for cadet officers at the United States Navy Academy at Annapolis. I had consciously sought to give balance to the novel, to show that there are always heroes on both sides in every war - and the fact that both countries had officially found some educational value in the history-based fictional story was very gratifying.

I spent six months travelling to and from China and Vietnam during the first half of 1988, passing several times through Bangkok and Hong Kong as our film unit positioned itself back and forth between Vietnam and China. These first visits to Thailand inspired my next novel *The Bangkok Secret*, which was published in 1990.

My interest was quickly aroused on learning of the mysterious death of the nation's young King Ananda, who had been found dead in his sumptuous Bangkok palace in 1946 at the age of twenty, with a single bullet wound in his forehead. His full title had been King Rama VIII of Siam and the mystery of his death still remains unresolved. His brother Boomipol, then aged eighteen, succeeded him and remains on the Thai throne today more than half a century later, the modern world's longest reigning monarch. Again I researched the background deeply and built my fictional story around the mystery, without being able to present a conclusion that was beyond all doubt.

So in the space of the decade from 1978 to 1988 I had without any specific prior intention become fascinated by three of the world's most intriguing unsolved political mysteries - the death or disappearance of Thailand's King Ananda, China's Defence Minister Lin Piao, and Australia's Prime Minister Harold Holt. For a time I had considered taking the advice of others who said I should write the Harold Holt story as a novel. After deep reflection I felt the evidence of Mr Holt's clandestine activities was so strong and incontrovertible that it deserved to be presented as unvarnished fact. Perhaps in retrospect - the publishers in Australia because of the wave of media and government condemnation withdrew copies of the book from sale - I might have been wiser to present the facts via a novel. The story is certainly stranger than fiction !

In any event the most likely explanations for all these mysteries are discernible in one form or another in the books in question - and looking back, perhaps through investigating and writing about these mysteries I was unconsciously limbering up for a further climactic encounter with the most extraordinary unsolved mystery of them all on this planet: How did life here on Earth really begin? Who started it? When? Where? Why? - and of course ultimately beyond all that, the haunting question echoing down the years from my hostage cell: What is the Universe In ?

It is perhaps here worth drawing attention to the short linking passage to the last story in this book, *A Man Was Later Detained*, which is itself entitled: *No Story*. The short story is an ironic one about journalism and sub-editing and its introductory passage is deliberately based around the five basic and fundamental questions that fledgling journalists have been conventionally taught to ask and answer every time they approach and write a news story. The questions as I was taught them long ago are: What? Where? When? Why? Who? and in that introductory passage written in 1968 I concluded that in the most profound sense when addressing the matter of our existence in time and space, not one of those five vital questions could then be satisfactorily answered. Now, as I will explain later, I feel they all can be answered.

The Bangkok Secret was published in hardcover in mid-l990 by Macmillan and unprecedentedly Macmillan published a second novel of mine in the autumn of that same year, *The Naked Angels*. This second novel was a comic satire on sexuality and aging world leaders, based on the proposition that loss of sexual libido in later life can lead to erratic and dangerous decision-making by those with their fingers on the triggers of the world's most destructive nuclear arsenals.

The plot involves the kidnapping in turn of the President of the United States and the First Secretary of the Soviet Communist Party by the world's most alluring female guerrilla who has dedicated herself to re-awakening and restoring the lost sexual vigour of both world leaders in turn in order to make the world a safer place for all us to live in. I had written the novel several years before - in fact it was my second novel - and the unexpected ending of the Cold War with the collapse of Communism in Eastern Europe and the Soviet Union gave me the opportunity, tongue in cheek, to present it as the secret untold story of how that historic confrontation between the United States and the Soviet Union had been so suddenly and inexplicably defused. *The Naked Angels* is a very different sort of novel to those for which I had become best known and as its theme was not entirely frivolous I was pleased that it at last found its way into print

With those two novels out of the way I embarked in 1990 on my next major project, which I had conceived whilst writing *Peking*. I had decided then to complete a trilogy of historical novels set in the Far East by adding *Tokyo* to *Saigon* and *Peking*. Having at first hand experienced somewhat painfully what it was like to become caught up personally in the historical conflicts between Asia and the West - my two years as a hostage, it is worth remembering, was very much a result of Britain's past colonial domination of a weakened China, including Hong Kong - I came to feel it would be worthwhile in the third novel to illuminate through a fictional narrative the fierce enmity and distrust which had for so long characterised relations between the West and Japan.

I planned from the outset to cover a 150-year period starting in 1853, when the United States first clashed with Japan, and to end the novel in the present. This strategy in the event was to prove too ambitious and cumbersome for one novel and in fact I made slower than expected progress. After consultation with Macmillan they decided to turn *Tokyo* itself into a trilogy and publish its first part as volume one. Entitled *Tokyo Bay* it came out in hardcover in 1996 and in paperback in 1997. The second part of the trilogy to be entitled *Hiroshima* remains as yet unfinished in the year 2003.

The reasons for this are connected directly with that intriguing question which has now become the title of this book: What is the universe in? On the night of 8 May 1992 I began reading a very extraordinary book by a former French sports journalist and motor racing driver, Claude Rael. It had been sent to me that day by a female French business executive with Renault whom I had spoken to briefly a week or two earlier at a London seminar. We had exchanged business cards and without any warning she had sent me the book, which was called *The Message Given to Me by Extra Terrestrials*. It had been written and self-published in French by Rael himself some eighteen years earlier in 1974.

The book described in a matter of fact way a face-to-face encounter with the human male occupant of a landed UFO in a remote part of central France. Rael said that he was jogging around a volcano outside Clermont Ferrand on 13 December 1973 when the UFO appeared descending slowly and silently through thick mist. The individual who emerged from the craft was not much more than four feet tall although in every other respect he resembled an adult human male of Asiatic descent. He told Rael that he was the representative of an advanced extra terrestrial civilisation from outside our solar system calling themselves 'the Elohim' who had genetically engineered all life forms on Earth including us.

The scriptures of the Bible testified obscurely to this truth the visitor added, and in the past all prophets including Moses, Buddha, Jesus of Nazareth and Mohammed had been contacted and informed in a similar way by individual representatives of the Elohim who landed in extra-terrestrial craft. Rael was told that the various prophets had all been given insights and teachings to spread that were in keeping with the educational level of their particular eras - and now because scientific knowledge on Earth was sufficiently advanced, it was time that modern humanity understood the whole truth about the past and its potential future.

Rael described in the book how the UFO and its occupant returned for a succession of arranged one-hour meetings in a valley beneath the peak of the volcano on six consecutive days. Each time he wrote down in detail what he was told and after unsuccessfully approaching a number of publishers in Paris he eventually published the information privately himself in French in a book entitled *Le Livre qui dit La Verite - The Book Which Tells the Truth*. By the close of the final meeting he had also accepted the mission he was offered to make this new information known to the world.

Part of the mission was to begin the process of establishing an embassy for representatives of the Elohim, to be built with a rooftop landing-pad for their spacecraft in a neutral area preferably close to Jerusalem. There, Rael was told, they would be prepared to meet our world leaders and representatives of the international media. Rael's visitor predicted that such an open and official landing could lead to an unprecedented era of enlightenment and scientific and technological progress – a veritable 'golden age' on Earth.

It is impossible to summarise quickly the contents of *The Message Given to Me by Extra Terrestrials*. It is sufficient to say here perhaps that despite its highly esoteric nature I was profoundly impressed by the sheer logic and good sense of the entire book. In fact I read it right through the night of 8 May 1992 without sleeping at all and rose at the normal time next morning feeling elated at having stumbled across possible truths of enormous import.

About 3 a.m. the moment which this narrative has been leading up to, arrived. I had reached a passage where Rael's informant said in effect: 'We have proven scientifically that infinitely small matter is exactly the same as infinitely large matter.... Sub-atomic particles inside the cells of your body contain universes and galaxies and solar systems with planets supporting minute forms of intelligent life just like us. In turn our universe itself is also a sub-atomic particle inside an immense biological body of some kind. It might exist inside an arm or a leg of the great being. Infinity extends indefinitely in both directions, great and small.'

Reading this was for me a great moment of insight in my life. I sat up straight in bed (I was sleeping alone) and let out a whoop of delight, immediately recalling that I had written in that passage *What is the Universe In?*: 'The universe is *in* something! All life must be relative... one day far ahead... everything a million years old will explode in a shower of light and perhaps some unimaginably gargantuan figure in which the universe resides unseen will say to his equally gargantuan wife: 'Ouch! That pain I've had in my big toe recently just got worse....But now it seems to have disappeared completely !'

To read of somebody saying they have scientifically proved something without providing the concrete proof is of course by no means conclusive. Yet the logical and rational context of Rael's whole book provided for me an immediate and strong conviction that this definition of the infinite nature of our reality was a confirmation of the truth I had somehow stumbled on intuitively whilst held as a hostage over a long period in a state of solitary confinement.

In addition Rael's book provided what was for me the first truly persuasive explanation of our physical origins, our planetary history and our chronically divisive religious beliefs. For me it set our past present and future on a firm scientific basis - but without in any way diminishing life's joyous spiritual dimension. As I saw it, the book did not undermine everything from our past, it simply refocused understanding in a new way. After reflecting at length too, on the book's enormous implications, I felt it had the potential to help transform us and our world beyond all our previous expectations. Most importantly it provided a context in which the greatest and most intractable problems of our planet - constant warfare, disease, pollution, hunger, poverty, criminality - might be resolved.

After a few months, having read all of Rael's other books, I sought out members in London of the organisation that Rael had formed in the mid-1970s to help him with his mission, the International Raelian Movement. I had many questions and wanted to discuss them with people already familiar with Rael's writings. I joined the Movement to find out about it from the inside, to investigate it as a journalist, and met Rael himself for the first time in France two years later in August 1994. This was at a Raelian seminar and I recorded my first interview with him there. From the first meeting I felt convinced he was truthfully relating all that he had experienced.

I later recorded another interview with Rael which became part of an investigative series of radio programmes, which I was commissioned to write and present as an independent production for the BBC World Service Radio. The title of the series was *UFOs - Fact Fiction or Fantasy?* and the programmes were broadcast and repeated worldwide in 1996 and 1997. My researches, which took me to a UFO World Congress in Germany and to New York to interview leading experts in the field of alleged alien abductions, quickly convinced me of one important thing - that all major governments worldwide secretly recognise that extra-terrestrial craft of many different kinds come and go in our skies at will and have done for a long time.

The world of UFOlogy is also awash with countless rumoured stories of alleged past contacts between extra-terrestrial visitors and government representatives from various countries. It is impossible at present to know what such contacts have amounted to, if and where they have taken place, and whether genuine information about such things will be admitted and revealed in the near future. The balance of probability is that sooner rather than later the existence of extra-terrestrial races will have to be officially and publicly acknowledged.

Leaving on one side the worldwide reports of alleged abductions by 'aliens', a number of private individuals over the years in different countries have also claimed to have experienced benign encounters with extra-terrestrial visitors. Whilst a few of these claims have undoubtedly been proved fraudulent, it seems certain to me that at least some have been genuine. Nothing that has been reported, however, comes anywhere near the scope and scale of the experiences that Rael has described in such detail in a total of five books published in English to date.

Rael has unrelentingly pursued his mission 'to inform not convince' for three decades, travelling the world to give media interviews, lecture and teach the received philosophy and meditation techniques of the Elohim at seminars on all five continents. In December 2003 he celebrates thirty years of endeavour with the first worldwide gathering of the International Raelian Movement, which now lays claim to 60,000 members in more than 80 countries.

For two years from 1996 to 1998 I became the national president of the British Raelian Movement. During that time I re-translated Rael's first book from French in order to publish it commercially for the first time in English. To do so I set up my own new publishing imprint, The Tagman Press, feeling that it was vitally important for all Rael's books to reach a wider audience through the traditional book trade in the

United Kingdom and abroad. Until then his books had been published solely by the Raelian Movement and sold largely at its meetings and public events nationally and internationally.

Rael's first publication that I had read through that one night in May 1992 was redesigned and launched as a Tagman book in the UK in 1998 under the revised title *The Final Message* with the subtitle *'Humanity's Origins and Our Future Explained'*. Other titles such as *Let's Welcome the Extra Terrestrials*, *Sensual Meditation* and *Yes to Human Cloning*, have followed. To date Rael's books have been voluntarily translated into 24 languages by members of the Raelian Movement.

Since its inception, Tagman has gradually expanded to publish books on journalism, travel and self-development as well as books by other authors who also challenge convention in areas such as science, health and spirituality. Most notable is *Your Body's Many Cries for Water* by Iranian-born Dr Fereydoon Batmanghelidj, an outstanding health bestseller. In this book, which has overall sold half a million copies worldwide, the author proves to many people's satisfaction that dehydration is the cause of most major modern illnesses. Drinking eight glasses of water a day, says Dr Batmaghelidj, can restore, improve and protect any individual's health. He castigates the multinational pharmaceutical companies, saying they kill far more people each year than international terrorism - and he says the swig of water we take to swallow pharmaceutical drugs does us much more good than the drugs themselves. He has also written books on back pain and asthma, citing dehydration as a prime factor in both afflictions. I strongly support his efforts to get governments worldwide to acknowledge his revolutionary discovery, which can radically improve healthcare everywhere and potentially make enormous savings in government health budgets.

In December 2002 The International Raelian Movement and its leader became the focus of worldwide media attention in an unprecedented fashion. Two days after Christmas, an announcement was made by Dr Brigitte Boisselier, the Raelian president of a company called Clonaid which Rael had set up in 1997 to help infertile couples have children following the successful first cloning of Dolly the sheep.

Dr Boisselier told a packed press conference in Miami, Florida that Clonaid had helped an American woman produce the world's first cloned human being, a little girl called Eve. Later four more cloned births were announced by Clonaid in other countries. The absence however of any clinical or scientific evidence from Clonaid that the babies were truly clones, has led to outpourings of scepticism in news media worldwide about whether the company's claims can be trusted or whether the announcements were contrived simply as a publicity stunt.

What is incontrovertible is that Rael has been speaking of genetic engineering and cloning since 1973. The resurrection of Jesus of Nazareth after his death on the cross, Rael was told, was made possible by employing a very advanced form of human cloning, involving an accelerated growth process. In the most dramatic moment of *The Final Message*, Rael describes how on the planet of the Elohim he watched an identical clone of himself materialise from a machine within minutes after a single cell sample was extracted from his own forehead.

So in my view it is clear to all who take the time to read carefully what Rael has written, that in setting up Clonaid he was pursuing his mission to draw attention to the extraordinary message to all humanity that he was given to deliver from a volcano in the Auvergne way back in December 1973. Whatever the outcome of the current controversy surrounding Clonaid and the first possible cloned human beings born via a rudimentary form of cloning, it is clear that Rael and his supporters around the world – myself included – will go on working to spread knowledge of that very important message. Although it is not yet universally seen as such, it is, I submit, a message of great positivity and a tremendous force for good, which can ultimately be of enormous benefit to all humankind - if it is sufficiently heeded.

Which brings me back again to that little linking passage *No Story* written in Peking in 1968 wherein I concluded that on the cosmic scale of things there were no real answers to those staple journalist's questions: What? Where? When? Why? and Who? we are.... But 35 years later for me at least all that has altered. We are now living through the most momentous times of change, understanding and insight in human history. In my submission *The Final Message*, *Yes to Human Cloning* and Rael's other books do provide definitive answers to all those deep and fundamental questions. At last, I firmly believe, they show us clearly What the Universe *is* In!

Rael's writings also offer explanations about much else besides that we have never fully understood before - about our origins, our relationship with creation, our essential human nature and our destiny as a planetary race.

I am not, however, suggesting that anybody should simply take my word for any of this. To make a mature and considered judgement about the enormous issues Rael is dealing with and the mission he was given, it is necessary for every interested individual to read carefully what he has written. During the past thirty years as he has criss-crossed the world patiently and good humouredly pursuing his task, he has very frequently been maligned in the media. This has more often than not spread scepticism about him and his work rather than stimulated a desire among uninformed people to investigate further what he is saying. Unfortunately the modern media because of its nature is more of a barrier to radically new information than the natural conduit that the public imagine it to be.

In the eight years I have known him, I have found Rael to be a gentle, humorous and sensitive man, possessed of genuine humility. It is very clear to all who know him well that he is motivated in his task by great compassion and love Yet although slightly built physically, he is also very energetic and extremely strong and determined mentally, deeply committed to bringing about peaceful revolutionary change in the way we understand our past, our origins and our potential future. He also sees his very difficult role clearly and in context.

'I am not important in myself, I am only the postman,' he once told me smilingly in an interview I recorded with him for a BBC World Service Radio programme, emphasising that it is the nature of the extraordinary message with which he has been entrusted which gives him his remarkable stature. For these reasons he deserves much greater respect at the hands of journalists around the world than he has generally received so far. Fortunately there are definite signs that this has begun to change.

When I first published The Final Message five years ago through The Tagman Press I wrote in the Introduction that I considered it to be the most important book to be published anywhere in the world for 2000 years. I stand by that statement even more firmly today. The year 2003 will remain notable in history for the controversial - and in my opinion reprehensible - invasion of Iraq by an international coalition of countries led by the United States and Britain. Consequently the threat of new wars, the potentially appalling renewed use of nuclear weapons and worldwide terrorism seem destined to bedevil the world indefinitely. In these circumstances the essential part of Rael's mission - to prepare the way for the open and official arrival on our planet of representatives of the advanced civilisation who genetically engineered all life forms here - becomes ever more important. He was told that this super-historic event could effectively end all warfare and unite the nations and races of our planet in an unprecedented way. Could anything at present be more vital? Is there anything more worthwhile to work towards?

For these reasons I feel it is more important than ever for the media and the public at large to give Rael, his mission and his organisation very serious consideration indeed. Then more people might realise that enormous benefits for us as individuals and as a planetary race can flow from this

For my own part I am absolutely convinced that Rael is the most important man alive today on the planet - bar none. Early this year the most intense wave of media attention of his life so far followed the December 2002 announcement that Clonaid, the company he founded, had helped an American woman give birth to the world's first cloned human baby. Rael's immediate circle of supporters and helpers in Quebec, Canada where he lives, insisted then that the many journalists who flocked there to interview him should henceforth address Rael and write about him as 'Your Holiness' or 'His Holiness.' In other words after thirty years of frequent media disrespect they were asking journalists to extend to him the open respect that is given automatically to established spiritual leaders such as the Dalai Lama or the Pope - or not be permitted to interview him at all.

Significantly a growing number of interviewers in different countries are now agreeing to this. Having myself arranged international press conferences and media interviews for Rael as his publisher in the United Kingdom and the Irish Republic and having sometimes watched him demonstrate great dignity and courtesy in dealing with unwarranted hostility, this is an important step towards Rael being accorded the positive global recognition he so thoroughly deserves.

These are momentous times of change in which to be alive. I personally feel very privileged that my past experiences have led me to this point where I am able to help communicate widely ideas and information of such magnitude and importance from such a unique source. To support His Holiness Rael in what he is seeking to achieve and in particular to be his publisher in English is for me exceptional honour. It convinces me anew that those long years and months that I spent in isolation as a hostage in China over thirty years ago, were not entirely wasted.

Norwich, England, Summer 2003

Books by Anthony Grey

Autobiography

Hostage in Peking (1970)

Short stories

A Man Alone (1971)

Puzzles

Crosswords from Peking (1973)

Novels

The German Stratagem (1973)
(first published as Some Put their Trust in Chariots)
The Bulgarian Exclusive (1975)
The Chinese Assassin (1978)
Saigon (1982)
Peking (1988)
The Bangkok Secret (1990)
The Naked Angels (1990)
Tokyo Bay (1996)

Non-fiction

The Prime Minister was a Spy (1983)

New revised editions published by Tagman Worldwide:

Short stories
What is the Universe In ? (2003)
(originally A Man Alone)

Autobiography
Hostage in Peking Plus (2003)
(revised Hostage in Peking)

Audio-Visual CDs, DVDs, Audio & Videotapes of ANTHONY GREY'S documentary films, radio programmes and a radio play

Investigative Radio Documentary Series
*Independent series produced for
BBC World Service Radio*
UFO'S FACT, FICTION OR FANTASY?
3 half hour programmes on audio tapes or CD
£24.00

**Television Documentary Films
written and presented by
ANTHONY GREY**

Return to Peking and Return to Saigon
(2 one hour films priced £25.00)
One Pair of Eyes –One Man's Freedom
(1 hour film priced £15.00)
The Lure of the Dolphin
(1 hour film priced £15.00)
Witness of The Long March
*(30 minute interview with
Alfred Bosshardt priced £12.50)*

**Radio Play
written and adapted from a short story
of the same name by
ANTHONY GREY**
Himself
(1 hour CD priced £12.50)

To order any of the above titles
call 0845 6444186,
fax 0845 6444187 or
buy online at www.tagman-press.com
email: sales@tagman-press.com

Acclaim for Anthony Grey's international best-selling novels

SAIGON

'One of the most memorable love stories of our time..With this novel Anthony Grey establishes himself as one of the finest storytellers plying his trade today..It's a book which no doubt will stand the test of time.'
West Coast Review of Books

'The author's professional involvement with South-East Asia makes this a blockbuster of unusually painful intensity.'
The Times, London

'By using a technique of historic progression, Anthony Grey does for the Vietnam wars what Leo Tolstoy did for the Napoleonic wars. Indeed this masterwork could well be called the *War and Peace* of our age.'
San Francisco Chronicle

'He is a virtuoso of the epic novel genre. Like James Michener and James Clavell, Mr Grey is a master storyteller. Unlike them, however, he has something pertinent to say and does so in distinguished fashion... *Saigon* is a novel of terrible importance.'
Kansas City Star

PEKING

'A magnificent epic novel of modern China..The book is worth reading solely as a factual reminder of the chaos and calamity of China as a quarter of the world's people struggled and suffered towards modernity in the stormy and cruel decades between 1920 and 1980.'
Toronto Star

'A moving, authentic, tautly written saga of forty years of blood sweat and tears.conveys brilliantly the workings of the Chinese Communist system in its dealings with foreigners and dissidents.'
Los Angeles Times

'Grey, a superbly accomplished writer, weaves a masterly tale of triumph and tragedy..marvellous detail, erudite, imaginative and instructive sequel to his previous best-selling novel *Saigon.*'
Western Australian

'Grey's depth of feeling makes *Peking* a compelling epic.'
Sunday Telegraph

Other books available from Tagman Worldwide
online from our website www.tagman-press.com
or via our telephone credit card hotline 0845 644 4186
(internationally +44 845 644 4186)

DR FEREYDOON BATMANGHELIDJ

Your Body's Many Cries for Water ISBN 0-9530921-6-X (paperback)
'As a result of my breakthrough in medicine, we are now able
to prevent or even cure most of the painful degenerative
diseases of the human body.'
500,000 copies already sold worldwide

Water and Salt : Your Healers from Within
ISBN 1-903571-23-5 (hardcover) and ISBN 1-903571-24-3 (paperback)
Dr Batmanghelidj's brilliant newly published (2003) sequel to his original
worldwide bestseller which promises to be equally popular in
demonstrating that salt, in correct proportions, as well as water is vital to
our health and well-being,

CLAUDE RAEL

The Final Message ISBN 0-9530921-1-9 (paperback)
Advanced scientists from another planet genetically engineered all
life forms on Earth including us - now they wish to return openly
and land at their own embassy to assist us.
Over a million copies already sold worldwide
in 24 languages

Yes to Human Cloning
ISBN 1-903571-04-9 (hardback) and ISBN 1-903571-05-7 (paperback)
Cloning will enable humanity to live indefinitely in a
succession of physical bodies into which memory and
personality will be successively transferred.

Let's Welcome the Extraterrestrials ISBN 1-903571-28-6 (paperback)
Representatives of the advanced civilisation, which created us, wish to
land soon at their own official embassy with extra-territorial rights. They
will only come if we understand who they are and wish to welcome them.

Sensual Meditation ISBN 1-903571-07-3 (paperback)
To awaken our minds we must first awaken our bodies through sensual
meditation - genuine meditation techniques taught to the author by the
advanced scientists who genetically engineered us.

AUDIO-VISUAL

The Final Message is available read on CD by musical acting star Glenn
Carter who played the lead in Jesus Christ Superstar on Broadway and in
London's West End

Six guided Sensual Meditations
ISBN 0-903571-21-9 are also available on a double CD set with voice
guidance and background music

Dr Batmanghelidj's lectures worldwide on **Your Body's Many Cries for
Water** and **Water and Salt : Your Healers from Within** are also
available on Video and Audiotapes and DVDs

For full details visit www.tagman-press.com